MY FAIR
LADY VET

MY FAIR LADY VET

•

Jeanette Sparks

AVALON BOOKS
NEW YORK

PRINTED IN THE UNITED STATES OF AMERICA
ON ACID-FREE PAPER
BY HADDON CRAFTSMEN, BLOOMSBURG, PENNSYLVANIA

This novel is dedicated to my husband Leonard,
who always believes I can do anything and is there to support me,
and to my family.

Chapter One

On her way home from work, Dr. Margo Fitzgerald felt slightly brain-drained after a busy day at the veterinary clinic. The cell phone beeped. She rubbed her temple with her free hand and punched the answer button. "Hello, Dr. Fitzgerald speaking."

"Oh, good," the familiar male voice said. "Glad I caught you. You're needed right away. I can't leave the clinic at the moment. Seems a polo pony wandered off and ended up in a gully over on the Circle G Ranch. It's near your place, if I'm not mistaken. The foreman indicated he would meet you at the gate. Okay?"

"Fine, Al. I'm on my way." She turned off the phone and tossed it in the passenger seat.

The Circle G Ranch bordered her family's land in the Southern California desert near Indio, home of the National Date Festival. A feud between the Circle G owner and her Irish grandfather had been smoldering for years. Having worked as a racetrack veterinarian, she had had her fill of bull-headed men.

Margo whizzed past her family's lush date gardens

1

and alfalfa fields, breathing in the fresh scent through the open window. She stepped on the gas pedal and the Cherokee shot down the country lane.

When she reached the Circle G Ranch turnoff down the road a couple of miles, she caught sight of a white Range Rover parked alongside the old rock gateway. A tall, broad-shouldered man, thirtyish, unfolded his long legs and climbed out. Unsmiling, his dust-covered Stetson pulled down low over dark eyes, he leaned back against the fender and touched the brim of his hat with his finger. "Afternoon, ma'am."

"Hello," Margo called through the window. "I hear you have a horse in distress." She slid off the seat, leaving the car door open, and hurried to where he stood.

He folded his arms across his broad chest, giving her a doubtful appraisal, while casually crossing one scuffed boot over the other. "You're not the vet, are you?"

"Yes, I'm Dr. Fitzgerald."

He adjusted his sweat-stained hat lower. "A lady vet. Who would have thought it?"

"Something wrong with that?" she asked defensively.

The man's hooded eyes scanned her jeans-clad legs before shifting back to her face. His keen gaze caused her pulse to beat faster before she regained her composure.

That's enough already! she chided herself. "Where's the horse?"

Amusement played around his mouth at her discomfort and was just as quickly veiled. "I'll take you there," he said. His eyes flicked down the road.

Margo raised her hand to shield her eyes from the brilliant sun while she scanned the dirt road that ran past the ranch's imposing Georgian-style mansion.

"Rebel's the name," he said. The timbre of his voice drew down, deep and rich, and his tanned face broke into a grin. He turned on his heel and opened the vehicle's door. "Climb in, Doc."

"If you don't mind, I'll follow." Did she detect a hint of a Southern accent? "Do you know if the horse is badly hurt?"

"Hope not. I tried to ease down in the gully with him but he got all excited and I was afraid he'd hurt himself. Started kicking and bucking like all get-out. The horse's owner is supposed to be on the way. Polo players!"

He didn't sound as though he liked them very much. Margo had her own opinion, thinking most of them were men needing to prove themselves, but she kept her view to herself and jumped back in the vehicle. She edged in behind the Range Rover. The man, apparently the foreman, tore off down the road past the mansion like banshees were after his tail-feathers, making her glad she wasn't riding with him.

The mansion, recently painted, looked as though it should have been sitting amid magnolias on a plantation in the heart of Dixie—not in the hub of the California desert. Folks made fun of old man Gentry's place, calling it "Gentry's Folly."

Margo followed closely while the man ahead sped in the direction of the picturesque Santa Rosa Mountains. The new Circle G's owner had recently made an offer on the Fitzgerald ranch. When Grandpa Fitz received the letter, he raised his hammy fist and swore, "Conspiracy! Old man Gentry said he'd get our land one way or another! Well, I outlived the ornery coot, didn't I?"

Together, she and her Aunt Hattie had managed to calm him down with a cup of tea.

Margo grinned. He could be an irascible old Irishman at times, yet nevertheless she loved him dearly. Hadn't he raised her since she was ten? But her grin slid away to a frown when she thought about his increased temper and forgetfulness.

Enough of worrying about him, Margo told herself. *There's a horse to rescue.*

Dust kicked up from the vehicle ahead and she found herself eating dirt before she rolled up the window. "Slow down!"

She pressed her palm hard on the car horn. With a bone-jarring thump, her vehicle veered over a pothole in the road. She clamped her hands down on the steering wheel until she had it under control.

And where did you get a name like Rebel? This is Southern California, not the Deep South, for heaven's sake!

Without warning, the man pulled over and came to a halt. Margo slammed on the brakes, nearly rear-ending him. He threw open the door and lunged out. In two strides, he reached with a long sinewy arm to take the medical bag she had been about to drag out of the backseat.

"I don't need any help, thank you," she said brusquely, holding on to the bag. "I can carry it myself." She'd be darned if he'd take her for some female weakling. Cowboys had a fixation about helping a lady. Still, she liked his offer.

"Suit yourself."

He turned away. Margo cast a sidelong glance at his broad back. Dust and dried mud covered his faded jeans and denim shirt. He'd probably collected it when he tried to get the polo pony out of the gully. She couldn't help but admire his concern.

"The horse must have strayed onto the Gentry property from the polo field nearby," she said.

"Yeah." He motioned to her and took off on foot.

She tried to keep up with his long strides. The man must be over six feet, and he wasn't very talkative.

When they reached rocky hill terrain, Rebel gazed over his shoulder at her. She had fallen further back. He waited for her to catch up, his eyes speculative, then scrambled over a boulder. Margo followed, hefting the medical bag precariously under one arm. She wished she hadn't been so quick to proclaim her independence and refuse his offer. By now the bag weighed a ton. They continued to make their way across uneven ground filled with rocks, roots, and gopher holes, then came out on the crest of a hill.

A horse's panicked whinny and stamping hooves alerted them. Margo's heart quickened. The animal sounded so terrified. She had seen frightened racehorses virtually kill themselves thrashing around.

"We're close, Mr. uh . . . ?" She squinted at him in the heat. Perspiration had popped out on her forehead.

The man grinned. "Name's Rebel." When she didn't comment, he said, "The horse is over on our right. Past those boulders." He led off, slipped on some shale, and had to put down a big hand to catch himself. The small rocks made the going difficult and she, too, slipped a couple of times before reaching the perilous gully.

He took off his hat and wiped his brow with a handkerchief, then called to a middle-aged man whose wrinkled face resembled a walnut shell. "Ed, how's the horse?"

The older man's handlebar mustache twitched over thin lips as he shook his head with a negative frown. "Glad you're back, Mr. Gentry." He hefted himself up from where he'd perched on the edge of the gully and dusted off his hands on his jeans. "You know how these danged-fool Thoroughbreds act up. This one's nervous as a spooked cat!"

Margo's mouth dropped open. So Rebel wasn't the foreman after all but the owner of the Circle G! Rebel Gentry! She rolled it around on her tongue, theorizing. He must be old Gentry's grandson.

"We'll get him out somehow," Rebel said.

Turning to him, she asked, "So you're related to Mr. Gentry?"

Rebel smiled. "His nephew."

"I see. Sorry about him passing away," she said, although she had hardly known the man.

There wasn't time for further conversation but she returned his smile and followed him. The gully was partly hidden by desert shrubs. She peered down at the frightened animal. The horse appeared to be wedged in deep, and her stomach did a flip-flop. How were they going to get it out?

"We need a miracle," she said grimly, laying the medical bag down.

Rebel nodded, his face stern. "The danger of a cave-in compounds the problem." He glanced around. "You can see the earth around here is so pocked with prairie dog holes that it's very unstable."

Margo nodded and started the descent without saying more, dragging the medical bag. She hadn't realized Rebel was inching along behind her until she heard him cough. The dust was thick.

"There's not enough room for the two of us," she said. "I've got to do this alone."

"Alone? What the Sam Hill do you think you'll accomplish?"

"There's no time to discuss this. Just let me do my job."

With a hard glint in his eyes that told her he wasn't used to taking orders, he mumbled an oath and backed away. Margo moved downward step by precarious step. The horse, a magnificent gelding, tossed its head in agitation, then shuddered. She kept her arms close to her sides, fearful of making a rapid movement, and spoke in soothing tones. The horse could rear up at any time and strike out with its powerful hooves.

"There now, big fella. Yeah, I can see you're in an awful predicament. Just keep calm. I'm here to help you."

Pure terror registered in the horse's eyes and quivering bulk. It tossed its handsome head, the long mane fanning out like a palm frond in the desert breeze. Slowly, she raised one arm and continued to speak in a hushed voice, moving closer all the while. Loose dirt and rocks lay littered around the horse's hooves. She grimaced, seeing the evidence of the gelding's attempts to escape the confinement of the blocked gully.

Margo quickly assessed the problem. The splendid creature sniffed the air, then allowed her to stand beside him. She gently ran her fingers along his dust-covered neck.

Taking a quick glance upward, a wave of claustrophobia washed over her, making it easy to understand how the horse must feel. Fortunately, the gelding hadn't broken a leg when he tumbled down to the gully floor.

Still, the possibility of internal injuries plagued her. She examined him as best she could in the confined space. Except for near exhaustion, he appeared sound.

Margo cupped her hands to her mouth and called up to Rebel Gentry. "Send down the canvases now, will you please? I'll make a sling. And would you bring back your biggest tractor as fast as you can? You'll need to pull him out pretty soon."

"Sure thing." Rebel stared down from above. He watched helplessly as she worked alone. Well, she was calling the shots, he figured, and he respected her efforts. But all the same he was reluctant to leave. What if something happened? Horses could suddenly do the unexpected.

Swearing under his breath, he motioned to Ed and they hurried off.

When Margo looked up again, another man with light hair peered down at her, grinning. She thought he must be the handsomest man she had ever encountered, sort of a younger version of the actor Peter O'Toole.

"I'm Kane Huntington, and that's my horse," he said in a British accent. The late-afternoon sun streamed around him like a halo.

"Why in blazes didn't you keep your horse corralled?"

"Sorry." The handsome face receded.

The horse's veined ears pricked forward at the sound of his owner's voice. He whinnied and made a half-hearted attempt to scramble up the side of the gully. She threw her arms around his neck. "Whoa!"

The air grew hotter as clouds of dust rose. The walls seemed to close in, sucking both her and the gelding farther down into the pit. She said a hurried prayer, opened the medical bag, took out a needle, and injected the horse with a mild tranquilizer, then stroked his dusty back.

Time seemed to drag on, and after a little while, she asked herself desperately why the men hadn't come back. Each second measured that much less light to work in, and she willed herself to keep calm.

Without any warning, the gelding bared his teeth, nostrils flaring, and tried to take a chunk out of her forearm. She flung herself back against the dirt wall, her heart racing. He shuddered, then slowly settled.

I need all the help I can get, she told herself. *That, and a lot of luck.*

Why couldn't the horse's owner lend a hand now that he was here? He was probably reclining up there sipping a cold beer.

"Hey you—the owner of this poor animal," she shouted.

The handsome face reappeared, all smiles. "His name's Phar."

"Would you please get down on your knees and start talking to your Phar," she ordered briskly. "He's plenty scared." *And so am I.*

The polo player raised his shoulders, conveyed a contrite gesture, then let his warm gaze ramble over her. "I'm so sorry to be all this bother. Of course I will be glad to do anything you ask."

"What's Phar mean?" she asked, curious in spite of herself.

"Phar Lap was once a great race horse here in California in the 1930s," Kane said. "He won a lot of races. That's why I named my horse after him. He's made me plenty of money too."

"I see." Kane seemed much too interested in the horse's value, she thought with disgust, but at least the gelding was less agitated after hearing his owner talking. Changing the subject, she asked, "Any sign of the tractor?"

"Not yet. By the way, my father told me he called you in recently when one of his horses became ill. He said you did a splendid job of patching the pony up."

"I'd rather you talk to the horse, if you don't mind." She was in no mood for flattery.

"Right." He followed instructions but spoke as though the act embarrassed him. "Hold on, Phar, my boy, we will be riding after the puck in a jiffy. There, there now, big fellow."

Margo stifled a chuckle at his attempt to sound jocular. However, the tranquilizer was beginning to take effect and the horse lowered his head.

"What's taking them so long?" she asked. "I can't see too well down here now."

"I'm afraid I don't know."

Just as she thought the tranquilizer was working, Phar lunged sideways, pinning her to the wall of the gully. The air went out of her lungs as tunnel vision set in.

Rebel and Ed worked together, hurriedly tossing canvases and horse coverings into the back of the pickup.

Rebel slammed the tailgate shut. "I hope the fool polo pony doesn't stomp that lady vet to death while we're gone. You take off now, Ed. I'll get the tractor."

Ed tipped his hat, then jumped into the truck. In seconds he was barreling down the road like a whirlwind.

Rebel sprinted to the barn, leaped up on the tractor seat, switched on the engine, and shot the machine backward out of the structure with a roar. Turning, he drove the tractor at its maximum speed along the rutted dirt road, weathering the bumps that vibrated up through his body.

When he reached the area strewn with boulders, he shoved enough of them aside with the scooper to get the tractor through and lay out a makeshift road. Ed was there waiting for him.

Back at the gully, Rebel hurried over to check on Margo. In the gloom all he could see was the horse's back. *Oh, no, where is she?*

A man stood looking down on the other side, and called over to Rebel. "The vet was talking to me and all of a sudden she stopped. I'm wondering if . . ."

Rebel strained for a glimpse of her. His heart did a double beat, thinking something was terribly wrong. "You okay down there?"

When she didn't answer, he dropped down on his belly and leaned far over. To his horror, he spotted her limp form wedged beside the horse, slightly under it. She looked like a dirty rag doll. "Oh, no!"

Without thinking, he lumbered up and vaulted over the side, landing on his feet just behind the horse. Fortunately, the animal didn't kick. Rebel had only enough room to reach down and snatch her from under the animal. Her face looked pale under a mask of dirt. He swept her into his arms, fearing she might have been crushed. She looked so fragile. He wondered how he was going to get her up to the top without harming her further.

Margo groaned, and her eyes flew open. "Put me down," she said in a weak voice, but she didn't struggle. "Did you get the canvases?"

He was so relieved, he almost kissed her honey-fringed eyelids. Instead, he gently set her on her feet. "We've got them. You okay? You gave me quite a scare."

"Sure, I'm okay—I think." She looked a little wobbly on her feet. "The gelding smashed me up against the wall. Knocked the wind right out of me. Thanks. Let's get a move on now. I'll make the sling for the horse. You start laying canvases down on either side of the ravine. If we're lucky, it'll help hold the dirt back when you pull him out." Rivulets of sweat made a path down her face and she tried to wipe them away, making her face resemble a marble cake.

"You're not going to do that all by yourself?" he said with a determined shake of his strong chin.

Her shoulders set stubbornly. "Yes I am! Don't you see, it's the only way. There's not enough room down here for us both to do more than turn around."

He swore, knowing she was right, but fighting it. He had a need to protect this woman, even if he wasn't certain why. "What if—"

"We don't have time for what if's," she interrupted. "Now come on!"

Reluctantly, Rebel agreed.

Chapter Two

"Turn the horse covers upside-down under the gelding's belly and fasten them as tight as you can across his back," Rebel told the lady vet.

"My thoughts exactly. Ease them down behind the horse's rump, along with the rope."

Her bossy tone irritated the heck out of him. Hadn't he just saved her hide? *Okay, lady, you're on your own.*

He hugged the side of the earthen wall and scrambled at an awkward angle up the side, barely keeping his footing. Ed gave him a hand over the top.

"What happened?" Ed said. The look on Rebel's face increased the lines on the foreman's brow.

"The doc's okay. Let's drop those canvases over the side before the horse causes more mayhem."

Dogged by a feeling of urgency, they dropped the canvases and set to work on their end. Rebel did a fast calculation of the horse's probable weight, knowing it was well over a thousand pounds. He hoped the tractor could pull the gelding free before the canvas covers came apart at the seams. The setting sun left little working time.

Down in the gully, Margo had her hands full. When she tried to fasten the first covering under Phar's belly, the animal shifted and attempted to buck. Why hadn't the tranquilizer been more effective?

She managed to slip one, then the other in place. The ticklish part came when she climbed onto his dusty back and leaned down. She held on to his mane and attempted to grab a piece of covering. It slipped from her fingers like so many grains of sand. She tried again, praying he would not shift and crush her head like a melon. This time she grasped it firmly.

Margo's second attempt swiftly became a nightmare when Phar planted his back hooves squarely on the canvas and refused to budge. She got down and tried to lift a leg. He finally offered up first one hoof, then the other, allowing her to slip the covering into place. Her own strength ebbed. She had to stop for a moment to catch her breath in the fetid quarters, knowing it was now or never.

"Come on," she muttered to herself. "Get a grip. This isn't over."

Hearing her own words gave Margo renewed strength. She tied the first rope around Phar's body behind his front legs at the withers. His eyes were dulled from the sedative finally achieving its effect, his legs trembling, and he permitted her to finish.

Now that the sling was in place, Margo hurriedly braided the straps through the ropes for extra support and uttered a deep sigh of relief. By now her entire body ached and throbbed with pain, but the apparatus seemed secure.

"Okay," she called to the men above. "I'm ready."

She tossed up the ropes with great effort. Rebel and Kane caught them instantly and carried them to the tractor.

Rebel came back to take one last look at the lady vet and the forlorn horse, and swallowed hard. At least the horse appeared reasonably calm now. However, its adrenaline would pump with renewed vigor when Rebel began to haul him out. He didn't want to think about what could happen. A horse's legs were fragile. After all this, he hoped the gelding survived. Yet the danger to Margo Fitzgerald unnerved him the most, and his stomach muscles squeezed down. He tried not to envision the horse's frightened struggling and what might happen if she got in the path of those powerful hooves.

Rebel climbed into the tractor seat, grumbling. He rubbed his jaw hard with the back of his hand as he switched on the engine.

Ed, who was watching the action below and acting as go-between for Rebel, nodded solemnly, circling his fingers in the "okay" position. Rebel inhaled and eased the shift forward. His hands gripped the steering wheel so hard his knuckles hurt and his mouth felt like a dried-up arroyo. He kept his eyes glued to Ed, who continued to nod in the affirmative.

As he slowly hauled back, an excitement replaced the churning in the pit of his stomach. The thought that he might actually get both of them out unharmed raised his anticipation to lofty heights. He glanced up momentarily at the twilight. "Please!" he murmured a prayer.

When Rebel saw the horse's head, followed by the big hairy back, come out of the gully, he took in a sharp breath. Then Margo appeared. He let out a whooping yell of satisfaction as Kane eased her over the embankment.

Margo stretched, gulped in fresh air, and had a coughing fit. Having reached terra firma, the horse slowly rose and got up on all fours, shook himself like a giant dog, and snorted. With a pathetic droop of the head, he let out a low nicker. Margo and Kane unfastened the horse covers, letting them fall to the ground in a heap. Phar stepped stiffly over them. Rebel sat on the tractor, momentarily drained, watching the scene unfold. He had to hand it to Margo Fitzgerald.

Kane gave his horse an affectionate pat on the withers. "Doctor, you are a wonder!" he said.

But by now the lady vet looked as though she could chew nails, Rebel thought, as he switched off the tractor engine.

Unfazed, Kane went right on with his palaver. "Oh, you are something else—an angel in disguise! Will the horse recuperate—be active again, I mean?" He looked hopeful.

"That depends if he has any serious injuries," Margo said, her voice decidedly cool. She examined the scratches on her own hands and the broken fingernails. "I think he'll be all right." She thrust her hands in her jeans, wincing at the pain.

Dr. Albert Thornsey, the veterinarian Margo worked with, had arrived just minutes before Rebel freed the horse. He smiled his approval and gave Phar a cursory examination. "You did just fine, Margo. But we'd better take the gelding back to the clinic and X-ray him just to be on the safe side. He does have sizable contusions on both kneecaps. I'm sure Kane, here, agrees."

"Of course," Kane said with an ingratiating smile.

Margo nodded, then ran her tongue over her dry lips. "It was touch and go down there, Al. I thought the covers might split with his weight but they held, thank goodness."

Kane turned to a distinguished-looking man dressed in jodhpurs, grinning. "Dad, she did it."

The man's gray hair shone like quicksilver in the twilight as he stepped forward. "We were all counting on you, Dr. Fitzgerald," he said in a clipped British accent. "You certainly have a fine way with horses. Everyone in the valley says so."

Margo recognized Bradford Huntington, the owner of the polo field. He, too, had recently made an offer on the Fitzgerald ranch, a paltry sum at that.

"Thank you. This horse is from your place, then?" she inquired, knowing full well where the animal came from.

"Yes, I am ashamed to say." Huntington groaned and glanced over his shoulder at his son. "Kane left Phar in the paddock after playing polo this afternoon. One of the grooms was supposed to give the gelding a cooldown walk. I guess he became involved with something else and neglected to close the gate. We are just over the sand dunes, you know." He pointed in the direction of the polo field that lay only a couple of miles from both the Circle G Ranch and the Fitzgeralds' Desert Jade Ranch.

Margo brushed vainly at her blue jeans. "Seems to me you ought to find better help. It's a wonder the horse didn't get killed." *Or kill me.*

The older Huntington glanced down at his fine English boots, apparently not liking her reprimand. She looked up to see a horse trailer arriving. Her gaze momentarily fastened on Rebel Gentry, who was still sitting on the tractor, and their eyes locked. Why had she been so rude to him when they were in the gully? He had only been trying to help her. Well, he probably had the impression she was a bossy know-it-all by now.

Rebel's face broke into a broad grin. She gave him a weak smile in return before shifting her attention to the men loading the polo pony in the trailer. Rebel put on the emergency brake and jumped down, then ambled over to lend a hand. Giving the gelding's rump a shove, the horse entered the trailer, and the men hurriedly closed the gate, bolting it.

Clearing his throat, Rebel spoke to Margo, who stood on the sidelines. She looked drained. "You must be exhausted, but you did a great job."

Margo's eyes lit up and she smiled warmly at him. Kane, however, broke in before she could reply. "This certainly calls for a celebration party. It isn't every day I have one of my horses rescued by such a beautiful woman. It will be in your honor, Dr. Fitzgerald."

Margo's brows drew together in a distinct frown, and Rebel could see she was about to refuse.

"Not so fast," he piped in, turning to Huntington. "The horse got lost on my property—right? If it hadn't been for Ed, who found him, you'd have a dead horse, Huntington. We'll have a barbecue all right, but right here at the Circle G."

He glared at the polo player for having caused all the problems of the last few hours, daring him to argue. Kane didn't. Although Rebel had a few choice words for him, he decided to keep them to himself. After all, it was over now and the horse appeared to be unharmed. He wasn't so sure about the lady vet.

Margo swallowed some of the dust in her throat. "I think you did an outstanding job, Mr. uh, Rebel." The thought of a shower and bed seemed awfully good, and a party was the furthest thing from her mind.

"Thanks, but it was nothing," he said in a soft Southern drawl, shifting his stance. "I wish I could have done more."

Now that she had time to think of something other than the horse's welfare, she let her mind soak up the fact that Rebel owned the Circle G Ranch. He apparently knew what he was doing. Folks in the valley talked about how the ranch was thriving again.

Stretching to his full six-foot frame, Rebel said, "We'll throw the barbecue this coming Saturday night—okay?" He kept his attention on Margo for confirmation.

"Okay. Thanks for the invitation."

He remembered that her hair was a ginger color under the coating of dust, but it was too dark now to see her face clearly. He turned to the others who were getting ready to leave. "You're all invited. Saturday at seven. Bring your families and friends. Everyone's welcome at the Circle G."

Chapter Three

The next morning when she came down for breakfast, Margo thought about Rebel Gentry's offer. A barbecue might be fun. Besides, she felt no animosity for the Gentrys, even if her grandfather still sported a long-standing grudge against a dead man.

Grandpa Fitz was in the midst of finishing his scrambled eggs when she told him about their being invited to the Saturday party. He shoved the plate away, glowered, and raised his white head like an old lion about to roar.

"You're invited too, Grandpa," she said, taking a seat.

"Never!"

"Why must you be so unreasonable?"

"I will not set foot on the Circle G! Not at all, at all! Stay away from there, girl."

Hattie, her unmarried aunt, stood at the ironing board performing her weekly ritual. She smoothed Grandpa's shirt, jerking a corner into place.

Margo turned to her. "Hattie, how about you?

Her aunt hedged. "I'm so busy, hon."

Ever since Grandma Mary died, Hattie spent most of her time catering to her father's whims, acting more like his mother than his daughter. She rarely went out and didn't seem to care about what she looked like anymore, preferring to wear her hair in a washerwoman style pulled up and fastened on top.

Before coming downstairs, Margo had called Julie Baker. Julie was her childhood friend, who'd recently moved back to the desert after a messy divorce. Always one to love a party, she'd jumped at the invitation.

"Mark my words," Grandpa Fitz growled, bringing Margo back from her thoughts, "no good will come of mixing with the likes of those lowlifes."

"Grandpa, we'll talk about it later." Margo sighed, still feeling the muscle strain from the day before. "I'll be in the study if you need me. Then I'm going to work."

"There'll be no more said on it," he shouted at her back.

Margo carried a cup of coffee down the hall. The ranch books, tossed on the top of the desk, were in desperate need of a going-over. Her grandfather had left them in a mess, not paying bills or entering those he did pay. She fought back the urge to give in to despair, and instead turned her thoughts once more to Rebel Gentry. His strong masculine presence there in the gully had been a comfort when deep down she wasn't sure she could accomplish the task of saving the horse's life.

Grandpa Fitz was going to be a problem over this one. Maybe she ought to call Rebel and give him some excuse for not attending. She loved her grandfather dearly, and was proud of him, but he could be a trial. A descendent of Irish farmers, he took great pride in what he'd built. Now, with his decline, everything was changing.

Like some giant carnivore, the looming taxes were a threat to their security, and the Fitzgeralds simply lacked the revenue to pay. That meant making the rounds again to see about a loan. Two banks had turned them down flat. Would she have had better luck if she were a man? Probably.

Margo took up a ledger. She'd taken over most of the farm's management, and her two jobs made life maddening at times.

Hattie came into the study carrying a basket with freshly ironed laundry and deposited it on a chair. "He gets ornerier every day," she said. "And more forgetful. I don't know what to do with him."

Margo nodded. "Come to the party, Hattie. You'll enjoy a night out. Please."

"My word, you sound like you're ten years old again. Why do you want *me* to go? I've got to see to your granddad. Besides, I don't have time to waste going to parties." Hattie's broad hands went to her hips.

Margo folded the ledger and dropped it in her lap, trying to come up with a more persuasive argument, when she caught the little twinkle in Hattie's eyes.

"Besides," Hattie said, "I don't have any party clothes."

Margo brightened. "You don't need to dress up for a barbecue—and I'll fix your hair."

"What's wrong with my hair?" Her eyes narrowed.

"Nothing." *Oh-oh, don't get her dander up now.*

Hattie pulled a face. "I like my hair just the way it is. It's neat. If you're embarrassed by the way I look, I'll stay home."

"Then you'll go? Wonderful!" She jumped up and hugged her aunt.

"If you insist." Hattie sighed deeply, as though the act of admission caused physical pain. "But it's against my better judgment. I know I won't have a good time."

On Saturday evening, Julie arrived a few minutes before 7:00. Margo opened the weathered entry door to the Fitzgeralds' low-slung adobe. Inside, the walls were thick and cool.

"Hi. I'm not too early, am I?" Julie asked.

Margo gave her an air-kiss on the cheek and drew her inside, giving her the high sign and speaking just above a whisper. "No, you're not too early. Hattie's still dressing. She had a big squabble with Grandpa, and he's sulking in his bedroom. He won't go with us, and he doesn't want us to go either. Same old feud."

Julie pursed her lips. "I'm glad you're not letting him get his way. I remember how he was when we were kids. I don't mean to offend, but you know I'm right."

"Come on into the living room," Margo said.

Julie followed and took a seat by the fireplace, crossing her shapely legs. She picked up a farm magazine and thumbed through the pages with little apparent interest.

"I'm glad you're back in the valley," Margo said. She recalled the fun, the confidences, and even the tears they had shared in the past. "How's the new job?" For some unexplainable reason she felt too nervous to sit down. Images of Rebel Gentry flashed through her mind-his smile, the way he held her in his strong arms in the gully, the tilt of his chin.

"I'm glad I went to work for Jonson Enterprises,"

Julie said, intruding into Margo's reverie. "The owner's son, Michael, is very good-looking." She dropped the magazine back on the coffee table and examined her coral-painted fingernail with the imprint of a humming-bird. "He said they're going to make you a second offer on the ranch—up the ante. Why don't you talk your grandfather into selling this place? You could get out from under your debts and move to a nice housing tract in town."

Margo couldn't keep her brows from flying together like thunderclouds and she shook her head vigorously. "Never! And it disturbs me that our financial problems must be floating like so many little dust particles in the valley." She certainly hadn't mentioned them to Julie. Maybe their date crop had been a bust last season, but she'd fight any developer's idea to pull down those precious date trees in order to build more condominiums. "Look what's happened to the valley already. Appalling. There're tracts everywhere now."

Perhaps her grandfather was right, and some sort of conspiracy was in the works. Three offers in a month did seem excessive.

Rebel Gentry had stated in his letter he wanted their land to increase his vineyards. Bradford Huntington, Kane's father, made it perfectly clear he wanted their alfalfa acreage to create another polo field to attract the international set. He reminded them that Prince Charles had come to the valley to play polo several times. Then there was Jonson Enterprises' miserable offer. She knew exactly why they wanted the land. A horrible vision of the Desert Jade being carved up three ways puckered her mouth as though she had bitten into a sour lemon.

"Hello again," Julie said, interrupting Margo's grim introspection. "You look positively lost in thought."

"Ah . . . I'm sorry. I was thinking about what you said. You know this ranch is never going on the market."

"But what if you can't pay the taxes?"

Margo bristled. "Ranching is a tough business, but we'll find a way. We always have."

Julie ducked her head and hastily changed the subject. "I heard in the beauty shop this morning that Rebel Gentry is one of the best-looking men in the valley." Her eyes danced merrily and she cocked her attractive blond head to one side.

"Well? What's your opinion?"

Margo smiled, pleased to be off the subject of the ranch. "I guess you can say he's nice-looking. Sure."

She remembered her friend's proclivity for attracting men. Julie would undoubtedly try to add Rebel to her list of admirers. The white linen dress she wore showed off her slim figure to perfection. In their youth Margo had been secretly jealous of the way the boys flocked to Julie. But now she had outgrown that worrisome frailty—well, almost.

"Come on, Margo, admit it," Julie said, grinning devilishly. "Rebel's made a powerful impression on you. Hope he doesn't have a wife and six kiddies."

Just then, Hattie came nervously through the door, with Grandpa Fitz barking at her back.

Over at the Circle G, Rebel and Ed Granger, his foreman, welcomed guests at the front entrance to the open double doors. Ed stood there fidgeting, stuck a hand in his pocket, and jingled some coins. Rebel had decided to invite a few ranchers in a payback effort. On several occasions they had invited him to social functions. For a while he thought of himself as the eligible bachelor of the month. He soon learned to decline, hoping to escape the eager matchmakers.

Maybe someday he'd marry, he told himself half-heartedly, gazing admiringly at a striking redhead on the arm of Bradford Huntington. She sashayed past him with a capricious grin. Since breaking up with Roxanne Humphreys, his fiancée in New York, Rebel had grown ring-shy. He wondered how someone he once thought beautiful could suddenly become unattractive. And why hadn't he seen earlier that they had nothing in common? It was a trifle late to be pondering these questions now, though, he figured. Roxanne may have been the wrong woman but it didn't prevent him from getting lonely for a woman's warmth sometimes.

Rebel turned back briefly to scout the large living room. Michael Jonson, his developer friend, leaned against the fireplace, already in vigorous conversation with Bradford Huntington and his young wife. Rebel grinned, wondering if Michael might be attempting to talk the Englishman into selling his polo field. Probably.

When he turned around, Margo Fitzgerald, the veterinarian, was coming up the steps toward him with two other women, and he felt a smile work its way across his face.

She thrust out her hand without hesitation. "I'm Margo Fitzgerald—remember me? This is my Aunt Hattie, and my friend, Julie Baker."

Rebel took a deep breath before replying. "I could hardly forget you. Glad you all could make it on such short notice. But I always say impromptu gatherings are the most fun, don't you?" He brushed his lips lightly across her cheek, finding her skin soft and warm, and liking the subtle hint of her perfume.

The women murmured in agreement, but he cared only about Margo's reaction. She gave him an inviting, genuine smile, and he thought he detected a touch of reserve or shyness there.

"Won't you come in?" He meant to say it gallantly but the words came out a trifle strained. Why did this woman make him feel less sure of himself? Her ginger-brown hair had been twisted becomingly into a French braid that hung slightly down her shapely back. He wondered what it would look like free around her shoulders, and he almost reached out to untie the emerald-green ribbon binding it.

Margo gazed up at him, as though she didn't quite understand what his hesitant expression meant. He noticed the hint of cinnamon that tinged her hazel eyes, the generous curve of her mouth, the gentle way her neck curved down into her lovely shoulders.

Ed coughed. Rebel turned, embarrassed that he had forgotten his foreman. "This is Ed Granger."

"We met out at the gully," Margo said. They shook hands. "Nice to see you again."

Ed nodded, ran the top of his boot behind his calf, polishing off imaginary dust, and held out his leathery hand to the other women too. "Welcome, ladies."

Hattie flashed the foreman a knock-your-socks-off smile, astonishing Margo. Her aunt looked nice in a dress she usually reserved for Sunday Mass. Hattie had allowed Margo to curl her hair, pull it back with silver combs, and add a touch of makeup.

"My niece told me how you found that horse," she

said to Ed in her plain-speaking manner. "Good thing you happened to come along."

He grinned. "That polo pony was plenty scared."

Rebel cleared his throat, patting Ed on the back. "Yeah, no telling what would have happened if he hadn't."

Ed kept his eyes on Hattie. "But your niece, here, gets all the honors for saving the gelding. Got right down in the gully with it." Then turning his attention to Margo, he said, "You're a brave little woman."

"That's kind of you to say but not true at all," Margo insisted. "Rebel actually saved him."

Rebel was too bemused by her sincere tone to argue further with the delectable Margo. He found her captivatingly attractive. "Mustn't keep you ladies standing here on the doorstep. Ed'll show you around." He started to move back. "On the other hand, I'll do the showing."

Margo wrinkled her nose, putting out her finger for emphasis. "You pulled the horse out," she said, stubbornly determined to give Rebel the credit. "I merely checked him for injuries and—"

"C'mon now, Margo," Julie interrupted, chuckling. "Let's go inside, for heaven's sake. You two can argue over who did what later on." She shot Rebel a saucy grin.

Margo smiled sheepishly, dazzling him. Feeling foolish, he stepped aside, letting the three women pass, and followed them into the foyer. Margo moved with a quiet grace, her head held high. Julie Baker whispered something in her ear, and he heard Margo laugh. The sound reminded him of a gentle mountain breeze stirring leaves. Someone tapped him on the shoulder.

Michael Jonson, his friend, stood there, a broad grin on his tanned face, and demanded an introduction to "these lovely ladies."

In no time, Michael and Julie fell into a lively conversation. *Small world,* Rebel thought. Michael was actually her employer.

When Rebel turned back, Margo had disappeared. Glancing through the crowd of people, he spotted Ed near the open French doors, his mouth moving at an animated velocity while he had Hattie Fitzgerald's complete attention. Just then Rebel's bloodhound, Napoleon, padded in from the garden. Ed saw him too and scrambled to grab his collar before the dog could lick someone's hand.

"Sorry," Ed called to Rebel. "Locked him in the bunkhouse but he must have jumped through the window again. Durn hound!"

"Let him be, Ed."

His foreman shrugged and turned back to Hattie.

Rebel slapped his thigh lightly, calling the dog to his side. Just then Margo moved dreamily into view. She was on the patio near a potted palm, resting her weight on one hip, chatting with Kane Huntington. Given the chance to examine her for a few moments without being observed, Rebel watched how she talked with her hands, and he found himself downright smitten. Then she stood quite still, discretely sipping a lemonade, her eyes focused on Kane. He must be telling her something awfully interesting, Rebel thought with a stab of jealousy. Kane wore a felt gamblers-style cowboy hat at an odd angle and looked like a dude.

All of a sudden Margo chuckled. Rebel frowned, wondering dismally if she found the Englishman attractive. He guessed women would call the guy handsome. Rebel didn't waste any more time but made his way through the guests. Napoleon followed at his heels like a furry shadow.

"Having a nice time?" He gazed deeply into Margo's eyes, and ignored Kane.

"Yes, thanks. We're talking horse-talk," she said with a cheery smile. Seeing the bloodhound, she bent down to pet the dog affectionately behind his long ears. "Who's this?"

The dog responded by giving her hand a wet slurp.

"Napoleon's his name," Rebel said. "Belonged to my uncle." He reached down to run his palm over the dog's smooth brown back. Napoleon turned up his drooping eyes.

"I think some eye ointment would help his eye condition," Margo said.

"Didn't know he had a problem." He took a closer look.

"I'm afraid so. Bring him by the clinic and I'll give you some medicine."

"Thanks. I will." He liked having an excuse to see her again.

"Nice dog," Kane declared indifferently, taking a swig from his tall glass. "Rebel, what do you think is the most adaptable horse for the desert? We were arguing the point."

Rebel thought for a moment. "An Arabian. Yeah, it would have to be an Arabian. They were bred for desert travel. What do you say, Margo?" He smiled at her, wondering if she would agree.

Margo thought for a moment. She was growing tired of Kane's charming banter. Rebel Gentry's intense eyes, as blue as the Mediterranean sea, left her slightly breathless. She had never been so attracted to a man in her entire life and wasn't sure she like the sensation.

"I'm sure you're right," she said to Rebel, and turned her gaze away, clearing her throat.

"Ah," Kane said, visibly disappointed, "a Thoroughbred any day."

Margo ignored him. She knew so little about their host. Grandpa Fitz thought all Gentrys were monsters. However, the more she was around this Southerner, the more she liked his offhand manner. The hound slumped against Rebel's long leg and stretched out on the patio.

Rebel smiled. "I've been thinking of raising Arabians myself. Maybe in the fall."

Kane broke in. "Going to be a Lawrence of Arabia, are you?"

Rebel ignored the inane remark.

"If I can help you, let me know," Margo said impulsively.

To Rebel, her voice sounded like music. "I just might. Thanks." He gazed up at the sky. The glittering stars reminded him of a movie marquee's lights. He dropped his gaze back to her again, wondering at his romantic notions. "Enjoying the night air?" He couldn't get enough of her smile.

"Oh, yes. The desert's at its best in the spring when the wildflowers are in bloom."

Julie wandered over to them. "Love your party, darling," she said to Rebel. He reacted with a weak grin. She flirted with him right in front of Margo, but when he failed to respond, she moved on, laughing as though it were of no consequence.

Margo wanted to throttle her friend, but she tried to

set aside her irritation, thinking she'd corral her after a while and take her home.

Kane said, "Julie's right. Great party, old friend!"

Rebel's jaw worked. Margo sensed he resented being called "old friend" by someone he hardly knew. She glanced back inside the living room. "Your home is so comfortable."

"Glad you think so. My great uncle built this place in the Thirties."

He stretched to his full height. His broad chest and shoulders revealed a powerful body barely hidden underneath a western-style white shirt with mother-of-pearl buttons. Although he didn't have a Hollywood handsomeness like Kane, he possessed a decidedly masculine quality. Margo judged him to be a man's man— strong and used to being in control. That could be both an asset and a liability.

"Let me refill your glass," he said, taking it from her. "Lemonade?"

"I'll switch to iced tea."

He turned to the bloodhound and pointed a finger. "You stay put."

Margo noticed a rusty horseshoe nailed over a door— a good luck symbol. Although the house was Georgian in style, Rebel seemed to prefer a Southwestern look. Guests lounged in deep leather couches positioned on either side of the massive river-rock fireplace.

He returned with the glass and she took it, thanking him.

"Take a seat, won't you?" he said, eyes darting to a cozy corner across the room.

She slipped into a chair covered in an Indian-design pattern.

"There you are," Kane chimed, joining them, eyes looking a little glazed. He dropped down beside Margo on a cowhide rug like an adoring puppy. The rug made her want to take off her shoes and run her toes through the caramel-and-white fur, except for him being there.

To Margo's annoyance, Kane kept gazing up and down her legs. She pulled the hem of her skirt down to her ankles.

"I admire the Mexican pavers covering your floors," she said to Rebel. "They glisten like rich spilled chocolate."

He nodded.

Bookcases lined both sides of the fireplace, with leather-bound law books and old classics sectioned from contemporary novels. The division revealed to her a love of order. Yet orderliness hardly went with a name like Rebel. She took a sip of her drink. Rebel's nearness stirred up a host of feelings and she found herself enmeshed in him, almost forgetting Kane.

"I'm glad you like my house," he said. "Not many frills here. My great-uncle never married."

She glanced down at his strong fingers. "And you?"

"I never married, either."

She tried to hide her satisfaction, admiring the sound of his deep, resonant voice, and the way his shirt tapered to a slim waistline.

"We'll be eating soon," he said. "Ed and the men set up tables on the lawn. I figured it was too nice a night to eat inside."

"Dining under the stars," Kane interjected with enthusiasm, waving an arm. "Sounds positively too romantic. Will you sit beside me during dinner, dear lady?"

Before Margo could reply, Rebel interrupted. "Sofia, my housekeeper, has already set out place cards. You'll need to look for your name."

"No problem," Kane said. He placed a hand on the floor and hefted himself up. "I think I'll go have a refill. Will you excuse me?"

Rebel tried not to look relieved, but Margo caught his expression before the curtain dropped. With the polo player gone, they both started to speak simultaneously.

"After you." Rebel gestured in a gentleman's manner.

"I was about to ask where you got your name. I hope you don't think I'm being rude, but Rebel is unusual."

A ripple of laughter emerged from his throat, along with a spreading grin. "My grandfather started calling me Rebel when I was a baby. Thought my colicky screeching sounded like a Southern rebel yell. Unfortunately, it stuck. My real name's Timothy. And since I'm not overly fond of that handle either, I found it easier to let folks call me Rebel. Of course, when I practiced law in New York, I got a lot of ribbing from the other lawyers."

"Ah, a little mystery unravels. I thought you might be from the South but I had no idea you were a lawyer." She took a sip of the iced tea and attempted to keep her voice calm. She felt a little breathless being so near him.

"You're right. I grew up on a plantation in Georgia. Is my drawl still so apparent?" he asked. "I thought I'd lost it."

"Only a little. I like the sound of it very much. How did you go from practicing law to ranching?" She sat the drink on a small table, giving him her full attention.

"Past tense. I'm not practicing now. You see, I inherited this place when my uncle died."

She admired the candid way he expressed himself. "From the South to New York to the California desert! That's quite a lot of territory to cover."

"Did you know him? He bought the land raw and planted table grapes. I guess he was sort of a loner. I only saw him a few times, myself."

"Sorry, we never met. My grandfather knew him, though." She fingered one of her silver earrings shaped like a miniature horse, declining to mention the feud.

"I understand your grandfather pioneered here in the Coachella Valley, too," he said.

Margo nodded, moving her body to the edge of the chair. Only inches separated them. "He came from Ireland and bought some acreage when he was barely twenty-one. Lived in a tent the first year." She chuckled. "He planted Irish potatoes but the prairie dogs ate them!"

Margo didn't know why she felt this urge to tell him her family history. It wasn't her habit to be a magpie, but he seemed genuinely interested. Perhaps it was because they both came from hardworking stock, connected inexorably to the land.

"So I see your family did some wandering too. From the green rolling sod of Ireland to the irrigated American desert. Admirable!"

"Do you miss practicing law?"

He glanced down at the backs of his bronzed hands, then across to her. "I prefer my close-to-the-land way of life. Actually, I planned to open an office once I got settled here, but now I'm so caught up in ranching I don't have time to even think about it. I guess the truth is, I've always liked working with my hands."

"You must have had loads of doubts." She liked the

way his eyes widened with interest when he talked about his work.

He smiled. "Whatever doubts I harbored have long since evaporated. It proved to be the best thing that ever happened to me—moving here—because it changed my outlook on life—the way I see the things."

She warmed to his frankness. "But it surely took a huge leap of faith to do it."

"Let's say I savor every day here in the valley."

"Me too." She smiled, feeling as though she'd known him much longer than a few days.

Rebel spread his forearms on the chair and shoved it back a few inches, stretching out his long legs. He thought about the time he had wasted trying to play New York lawyer. It wasn't what he'd really wanted—never could be. It had been what his father wanted. Here on the ranch he felt himself tested as a man far more than he ever did defending some corporate bigwig in tax trouble. Every day he battled with the desert in his impatience to produce the best table grapes in the valley. It meant sixteen-hour days sometimes, but it was worth every muscle strain.

He studied Margo's face, figuring she'd understand. Her eyes rested patiently on him. How long had he been reminiscing? He straightened, not wanting her to think he was losing interest in what she had been saying.

Margo nodded. "I totally agree—about living here, I mean." She pushed back in the chair until she felt the cushion at her spine and crossed her legs. "You must think I'm a nosy neighbor, plaguing you with all these questions. Well, I am."

Rebel grinned, taking his hands out of his pockets and covering his knees with his palms. "No way." He lumbered to his feet, towering over her. "I enjoyed exploring our family trees, but I think it's about time I gather up everyone and herd them out to the tables. You all must be starving. Thanks for letting me ramble on."

She laughed lightly. "You sound so enthusiastic when you talk about your ranch. I find it commendable. Maybe I can help round up your guests."

"Fine idea."

Rebel reached out to help her rise. He wished they could spend the evening right here—alone.

Unknown to Margo, he had already arranged for her to sit beside him at the big U-shaped table. He grinned, just thinking about the plan he had laid out so carefully.

Ambling to the middle of the room, he boomed, "Dinner's being served. Everyone hungry? Just follow me."

Margo wandered out into the garden, looking for her aunt and Julie. Still thinking of Rebel, she asked herself if he might be too good to be true. Hadn't he made it perfectly clear in his letter to Grandpa Fitz that he wanted their ranch?

C'mon, Margo, she admonished herself, *lead with your head and not your heart, and don't forget what Grandpa said about the Gentrys.*

Chapter Four

Rebel waited until almost everyone found their seats. Then, to his consternation, he caught Kane tucking Margo in beside his chair. *Wait just a minute,* he wanted to roar, *she's supposed to be sitting next to me!* But he held his tongue. Southern gentleman or not, he'd like to tell that polo player off right here and now! The man had the unmitigated gall to switch name cards.

Kane, the darling of the polo set, had pulled a fast one on his host, and Rebel couldn't do a thing about it without creating a scene. He smirked at the silly felt gambler's cowboy hat atop Kane's head.

Did Margo look a little disappointed that she wasn't seated alongside her host? Rebel hoped so. Julie Baker sat down at his right. However attractive, she didn't ring his bells the way the lady vet had.

A few seats further down, Hattie Fitzgerald grinned at Ed, their shoulders nearly touching. She methodically ran a napkin over a water spot on a fork. The act amused Rebel. To the left, just past Margo, Dr. Albert Thornsey and his wife were talking with Bradford Huntington and his young red-haired wife. He glanced back to Margo. Kane was chatting up a storm.

Sofia, Rebel's Latina housekeeper, had spread out barbecued ribs and chicken, along with a rich assortment of Mexican dishes, on the table, family style. The guests were industriously helping themselves.

A mariachi band gathered near the French doors, their voices rising in a melancholy love song. Except for the seating arrangement fiasco, everything seemed to be going well. Margo, however, continued to disrupt Rebel's peace of mind with the way she moved her hands when she talked or tilted her head when she spoke. He thought he detected a tired, even worried look in her eyes at times. Did she have a problem back home, perhaps? Maybe an important relationship had gone sour? But what did he really know about her? He recalled how exhausted she'd been after they rescued the horse, looking as though she needed a long vacation. Well, he'd love to fly her down to Ensenada, but something told him she wouldn't go. A woman like Margo Fitzgerald was never that impetuous.

Julie asked him a question about how to make chili and he turned reluctantly away from the lady vet.

"That's not in my department. Better ask Sofia. She's a pro," he said.

He realized Julie was only trying to make conversation, but he wasn't too adept at small talk.

Margo glanced up from her plate, and seeing Rebel in profile, smiled inwardly. She admired his strong, masculine face—the slight crook at the bridge of his nose. It crossed her mind that he might have been thrown from a horse at some time.

Kane nudged her elbow, grinning. "We must get together soon."

Margo gave him a faint smile. She caught the too-strong scent cologne. By now she considered him an open book, and his nonstop chatter had worn thin.

She caught Rebel staring at her, the corners of his mouth turned up pleasantly. Their eyes locked with a brief understanding. She tried to think of something clever to say but couldn't. An unexpected warmth coursed through her veins like a desert breeze, and it gave her a little shock to realize just how unstrung his attention could make her feel.

"Having a nice time?" he asked.

"Yes, thanks. This food is delicious," she said, thinking the remark sounded trite. She pulled her gaze away and shifted down to her plate, unable to go on.

"There's plenty more," he said, and reached across Kane with his long, sinewy arm to wipe away a smudge of barbecue sauce on her chin with a napkin.

Margo felt color rise from her throat to spread over her cheeks. "I hope you don't think I always eat like a pig."

Rebel chuckled, wishing he could hold her face gently in his hands and explore those unusual cinnamon-tinted eyes. "Not at all," he said. "Enjoy yourself."

He wanted to take her aside and ask her what troubled her, but sensed she was a private person. She had tentatively reached out to him earlier on, then drawn away like so much sand in his palm.

Someone called Rebel's name and he glanced down the table. Margo wanted him to turn his attention back to her but he didn't. Kane clamped his hand over her fingers, determined to be the center of her focus. She stiffened and tried to pull away, but he held on like an octopus until she gave a jerk.

"Did I tell you about my polo game today, Margo? I chalked up most of the points for the team. You told me to give Phar a good, long rest. I followed your advise and left him in the barn. Polo is such a physical game for both man and beast."

She nodded. "A wise thing to do. And yes, you did tell me about your game." She turned away and picked up her iced tea, sipping the cool, delicate beverage.

When the guests finished dinner and had dessert, Rebel stood up and smiled amiably. "I hope everyone's not too stuffed to dance. The mariachis are eager to entertain us."

He led the party, Pied Piper–style, toward the patio. The band strummed guitars and sang. Their big hats tilted back and forth in rhythm to the soulful lyrics.

Rebel found Margo clustered with some of the guests. "Enjoying yourselves, I hope?" he said to all of them. Then for Margo's ears alone, he murmured, "You seem more relaxed."

She gave him an odd smile. "Oh? I didn't realize I wasn't."

His heart lurched at the sound of her voice. "Want to dance?"

She smiled. "I'd like that."

On the patio, he took her in his arms. Her unusual eyes had already come very close to captivating him. She was light on her feet. The simple act of holding her nearly drove him to distraction. He knew he shouldn't be thinking these unrestrained thoughts but diverting them was like telling his hound not to scratch a flea.

Just then Kane tapped him on the shoulder. Incensed, Rebel wanted to ignore him.

"There you are, Margo. It's my turn." Cutting in, Kane took her hand with a charming grin, practically pulling her away from Rebel. "You know I've been waiting all evening—and you did promise."

She sighed, hardly elated. "Yes, I think I did."

Rebel caught the distinct hesitation in her voice and it made him feel good. He tried to keep himself from glaring at the glib polo player.

What a lot of hooey!

Kane had become a decided thorn under Rebel's saddle. He folded his arms across his chest, anything but complacent, his eyes firmly on Margo.

The Englishman wrapped his arm around Margo's slim waist and Rebel turned away, outwardly calm but agitated inside. He resented the man's monopolizing her. And when he heard Margo's peal of laughter, he rotated his shoulders back. Those two were suddenly acting much too chummy, to his way of thinking. He forced himself to go over and chat with a couple of ranchers, even though he kept one eye on the dancers.

After the song ended Kane asked for another dance but Margo begged off. She had promised Rebel another too. Not seeing him, she sauntered out onto the lawn for a breath of air. When she passed a part of the house with handsome French windows, she heard an angry male voice rise. From where she stood in the shadows, she could see half of Rebel's face. He was seated at a large claw-footed desk. His features were tightly drawn. Bradford Huntington and Michael Jonson leaned across the desk, their backs to her.

"Come on," Rebel said. "Didn't I make it clear? We'll get the land, believe me. Just don't go off half-cocked."

Huntington swore under his breath. "Boy Scout!" He scratched his ear. "I guess we can pick it up cheap enough at the tax sale."

Michael started to argue but Rebel held up a big hand. "We'll talk later," he said, stern-faced. "I've got a party going on, remember?"

Michael turned in profile and casually took out a cigarette. "Yeah, that pretty blond the firm hired is waiting for me."

Margo stepped back, her heart constricting her throat. Were they talking—plotting—to get the Fitzgerald ranch? She shuddered, her knees weakening. They had made independent offers but they could still be in cahoots, just as Grandpa Fitz said. Grappling with her emotions, she asked herself if this party might be a charade? She wanted to run away from the Circle G and the attractive man who now bewildered her. Yet maybe she was overreacting—reading something sinister into it when this private meeting didn't pertain to her. Other parcels of land were for sale in the valley. However, wasn't the Fitzgerald ranch centrally located to both Rebel's land and the polo field? Any illusions quickly crumbled.

Get real! she told herself. *You know exactly who they're talking about. Margo. my girl, you've been set up.*

Margo took off in a snit to find her aunt and Julie, bent on going home immediately. Looking around, she couldn't see either one. Rebel sauntered up, an arresting smile on his face. With effort, she forced herself to be polite, not wanting to give away or even hint at what she'd learned.

"You owe me a dance, remember?" he said.

Did his voice sound less gentlemanly? Could his appealing demeanor be some sort of grand coverup for his real mission? Maybe he thought he could persuade her to sell the ranch cheap if she became interested in him. He probably reasoned she wouldn't want to suffer the humiliation of having the property foreclosed on, either. Suddenly it all became clear. Yet she couldn't help feeling a twinge of regret.

Rebel stood waiting. Even though Margo wanted to give him a piece of her mind, she controlled herself. Better to play along, see what she could find out. Then again, what if she were wrong? *And pigs fly!*

"I have to go home now. Thanks for inviting me," she said, trying not to choke.

"So soon? Just one more dance, then."

"Afraid not. I have to get up early tomorrow."

Disappointed, Rebel's eyes lowered. Then Kane joined them before Margo could turn away, all smiles.

"You can't think of leaving, my dear Margo. It's early. We ought to dance until dawn," Kane intoned, slightly swaying.

"Tempting, but I can't. I need to find my aunt," she said, reaching for an excuse. "If I know her, she's probably sitting in a corner by herself at this very moment wondering where I am."

"Thanks for the dance," Rebel said, keeping his eyes on her and giving the polo player the cold shoulder.

A strained smile was all Margo could manage. "I enjoyed the party, Rebel. Good night, now."

She turned on her heel, aware of both Rebel's and

Kane's gazes on her. Why did she feel so suspicious just because she'd overheard part of a conversation? Where was the proof? She sighed deeply. Although she didn't want to believe it, the men had to be talking about the Desert Jade. Why didn't she just accept it?

Margo hurried back through the house, her head throbbing. Neither Hattie or Julie materialized. She started down a hall, just as her aunt came out of a guest bedroom, nearly colliding with her.

"Oh, there you are," Margo said. "Didn't mean to abandon you. I was—"

"Nice bathroom fixtures in there—real onyx," Hattie interjected. "I haven't danced in ages. Golly, I'm having a grand time. Hope you don't think I deserted you, sweetie. Are you enjoying yourself too?"

Her aunt looked positively radiant, contrary to what Margo would have believed. "Uh, yes . . . thanks, I am."

When they came back to the living room, Ed strode over. "Ready, Hattie?"

Without so much as a glance at Margo, she melted into his arms, and they danced across the floor to the patio, cheek-to-cheek in a sort of tango. Margo stood there gaping.

Kane, whom she couldn't seem to ditch, wandered up, holding a nearly empty glass. Giving her a crooked grin, he said, "Why don't you come to the polo game tomorrow? After it's over, I will take you to dinner at a little place near the Salton Sea. Fabulous view."

Margo hesitated. He looked so hopeful. Perhaps he might reveal something about his father's relationship with Rebel. Then she chided herself for being so underhanded.

"Promise me you'll come," he said. "It will be a great game and I'll play my best yet, just to impress you."

"I don't know, Kane. I've got so many things going."

"Now take a deep breath and say yes," he said in his most charming English accent.

She coerced a smile, feeling like doing anything but that. Yet the possibility of his knowing something intrigued her. "Okay, I'll take you up on it. And thanks."

"Until tomorrow, then. The game starts at one." Kane gave her a mock bow, his silly hat bobbing precariously, and moved away.

Across the room, Margo caught Hattie's attention and furiously pointed down to her watch. When she turned, Rebel was staring at her not more than two feet away. His forearm rested along the top of a chair as he lounged. "Before you leave, I want to have a word with you," he said.

What now? All ears, she wondered if someone had seen her outside his office. Then again, perhaps he was planning to confess his dealings with Jonson and the Huntingtons. Fat chance.

"You know a great deal about horses, Margo. I'm in the market for a good saddle horse," he began. "I'm afraid my ol' buckskin, Henry, is starting to break down. Would you help me pick out a suitable one? I'd pay for your time."

Her first instinct was an unequivocal no, but she thought again. Better to know one's enemies, someone famous once said.

"I'll help if I can, but I wouldn't think of charging you. Call it a neighborly thanks for inviting my family to your barbecue tonight." Then, meeting his eyes, she impulsively added, "Our ranch isn't for sale at any price."

Rebel smiled disarmingly, and for a moment he didn't speak. "Somehow I gathered that." He cleared his throat. "There's an equine auction next weekend. How about it? Can you come?"

"I think so. I'll check my calendar and get back to you."

His face broke into a lively grin, increasing the little crow's-feet at the corners of his eyes.

"Personally, I enjoy overseeing the vineyards on horseback, rather than in one of the ranch vehicles," he said. "Cuts down on pollution."

His dark blue eyes traveled down her body, causing her heart to flutter. "I really must go," she said. "Have you seen my friend Julie?"

"Hmm, not for a while."

She feigned a yawn. "I was up at dawn this morning. A heifer came down with colic over at the Zephyr Ranch." Then she smiled in spite of herself. "Thanks again. I've had a nice time."

She wanted to get out of there fast, away from his searching stare and his strong presence.

He frowned, taking her hand. "Just a nice time?" He waited, his eyes holding a challenge.

"Very nice," Margo corrected herself, withdrawing her palm. "I'll call you about the auction."

Getting a grip on herself, Margo walked away, looking for Julie. Her aunt was still dancing with Ed Granger on the patio, and ignoring Margo's entreaties. Hattie grinned coquettishly at her partner, her eyes glowing. She looked nice in the two-piece dress and the outdated spike pumps, Margo thought, hating to pull her away from an obviously enjoyable experience.

Margo decided to wait for the song to end out of courtesy before telling Hattie they simply had to leave. She hurried to the garden, hoping to find Julie. The mariachi band played on.

Floodlights attached high up in two Washingtonia palm trees lent a mellow glow below. At first Margo didn't notice Julie on the other side of a tree, but then she spotted her. Her friend was partly in shadow, engrossed in conversation with Michael Jonson.

Oh, shoot! How am I going to break in on this? she asked herself in total frustration.

The probability of Hattie and Julie wanting to go home now seemed zilch.

Someone touched her elbow. Startled, she jumped. Kane smiled down at her.

"Did I frighten you, dear lady?"

Not again! She shook her head, refusing to let him think he had. "I wasn't expecting you." He must think she went around spying on her friends.

"Why don't you let me give you a lift home?" he offered. "It looks to me like your girlfriend is all tied up."

His derisive laughter irritated her as much as his overly familiar manner.

"I brought my car," she said.

Julie and Michael looked over at them. "Oh, hi," Julie said. She ran her hand over her hair. Michael stuffed his hands in his pockets and leaned back casually on the two inch heels of his boots.

Julie giggled, her eyes glittering. "I suppose you're ready to hit the road, Margo?"

"Uh-huh. I'm getting sleepy."

The two men exchanged noncommittal glances.

"Okay with me. I've had a perfectly wonderful evening." She batted her long eyelashes at Michael and giggled again. He gave her a quick hug.

"I'll go find Hattie and meet you at the car." Margo wanted to escape Kane's good-night hug. He had that look in his eye. " 'Bye, Kane, Michael," she said, and didn't look back as she hurried back toward the house.

Margo caught up to her aunt. Hattie was standing alone, fanning herself by an oil painting of a pinto pony. Her blissful expression made her look years younger.

"Ed's gone to get me a glass of lemonade," she said in a fluttery, unfamiliar tone. "He's so nice."

"Hattie, we have to go now. Julie and I are ready."

"Well, I'm not!" Hattie shot back, glaring. Ed walked up and her mood changed faster than a roadrunner gobbling a worm. He handed her a tall, frosty glass.

Margo could almost see the wheels spinning in her aunt's head. Maybe Ed could drive her home? Her aunt took a big swallow, then handed the glass back to him with a sparkling smile. "I've had a very nice time, Ed, but the girls are ready to leave and I'll have to push on with them."

His rugged jaws dropped. "I was hoping you could stay for another dance, Hattie."

"Maybe I'll see you again sometime," she said. "Why, we practically live next door. Stop by for a cup of coffee any time."

Ed's face broke into a grin the size of a slice of cantaloupe. "I'll do that."

Rebel joined them and the "thank yous" and the

"good nights" started all over again as the party began to break up.

A few minutes later, Margo was finally heading home, breathing a sigh of relief. It had been an evening of discoveries and doubts. Rebel wanted their Desert Jade Ranch—had stated it plainly enough in the letter. And maybe, as Grandpa Fitz believed, he was in league with the Huntingtons and Jonson Enterprises to acquire the land one way or another. Like a fool, Margo had been impressed by the good-looking Southerner. Why did she have to overhear his discussion with the other men? Now she didn't know what to make of it.

Hattie groaned from the backseat. "My feet are killing me."

They pulled up to the house. The lights were still on, streaking through the windows like beacons. Margo put the SUV in park and they filed into the house.

"I'm going straight to bed," she said, knowing she probably sounded rude. "You know where the guest bedroom is, Julie. If you need anything, yell. I'll check on Grandpa. See you both in the morning."

"Well, I'll be," Hattie said, but she didn't go on.

When Margo peeked in on Grandpa Fitz, the lamp-light illuminated his grizzled face, revealing deep tracks of wrinkles on his cheeks. He slept on his back, snoring, his old red Irish setter, Beauregard, at the foot of the bed. The dog barely raised his head. She picked up a book her grandfather must have dropped and placed it on an end table, then switched off the lamp and closed the door softly behind her.

In her own room, Margo pulled off the tunic, slipped out of her skirt, and padded into the bathroom for a quick shower. The soothing water had a relaxing effect until her thoughts drifted to Rebel. His handsome smile floated before her in the steamy mist.

Rebel must think I'm an absolute ninny for the way I suddenly picked up and left. But I know what I heard.

Turning off the water, Margo stepped out of the shower and grabbed a thick towel, wrapped it around her, and began to brush out her hair. Then she pulled a white cotton nightie trimmed in lace over her head. Even though the clock showed half-past midnight, sleep eluded her. The shower had merely revived her thought processes. Not even the jubilant crickets chirping outside the window could lull her to sleep. Somewhere off in the distance an owl hooted several times, then grew silent, followed by a coyote's plaintive wail.

Maybe a glass of milk would help, she thought, vexed with herself. The house lay in darkness. She padded barefoot down the hall to the kitchen. The moon's silvery fingers slipped through the windows to furnish a shadowy light. She was about to flip on the switch when something outside caught her attention. Tiptoeing closer to the window, she peered out into the night. A figure carrying a lantern moved with measured steps among the outbuildings. Her heart trumpeted in her ears. The man was too short to be Ned, their foreman, and Ned never stayed on the ranch at night. She moved closer, her breath steaming the glass pane. He stopped dead, silhouetted in the moonlight, and riveted his head in slow motion toward the house. Margo stepped back, sucking in her breath. She knew her family frequently forgot to lock their doors. Was the back door unlocked now? Her grandfather's hunting rifle lay on a shelf in his room, and the .22 he had given her years ago for target practice was propped in the corner of her closet.

She took a step toward the door. Her heart beat so fast she could hardly get her breath. Was someone trying to steal their horses? And should she wake up her grandfather before taking action?

Margo ran to the door, and with trembling fingers, groped for the dead-bolt and locked it firmly. Then she remembered Hattie had already locked the front door when they came home.

Margo took another wavering peek out the window. The man had disappeared. Could he be hiding out there behind a tree? Picking up the telephone receiver, she hastily punched in 911.

Chapter Five

Sheriff Stoney arrived soon after Margo's call. A thin, wiry, middle-aged man, he had a habit of picking at a thumbnail. After a cursory investigation behind the house, he found nothing more than a few shoe and boot prints that could have belonged to anyone. Since nothing had been disturbed, he gave Margo a disinterested look and shrugged, took out a handkerchief, and cleaned his dark-rimmed glass.

"Doc, are you sure you didn't have a nightmare?"

She gave him a resounding "No! We came back from a party. I couldn't sleep, and . . ." To her dismay, he leaned closer and sniffed her breath, as though testing to see if she'd been drinking.

Hattie, having heard the sound of the sheriff's vehicle speeding up the drive, joined Margo in the kitchen, her eyes ablaze. Neither Grandpa Fitz nor Julie were disturbed by all the commotion, and Margo decided not to wake them.

After the sheriff left and Hattie made them a cup of

chamomile tea, Margo said, "Whoever the intruder was, he must have seen me and taken off."

"Do you suppose someone just wanted to frighten us?" Hattie grimaced. "Oh, I've been listening to Daddy too much, I'm thinking."

"I was petrified with fear. And to think Grandpa's dog never even growled."

Hattie nodded sympathetically. "He's getting old. Probably didn't hear a peep. Finish your tea, hon. We both need some shut-eye."

Hattie went off to bed and Margo didn't stay there long, apprehensive about being alone. Yet dropping off to sleep didn't come easily. She became aware of every creaking board and slanting shadow. The wind came up, sending furtive phantoms and whispers through the date trees in the grove outside.

The following morning Julie set flatware on the kitchen table and listened to Margo's and Hattie's accounts of the previous wee hours of the night. "Why didn't you wake me? I missed all the fun, darn it," she said.

"Thankfully it turned out to be nothing serious," Margo said. "He was probably an illegal immigrant trying to spend the night out there before heading for some city. It's not the first time it has happened."

She helped Hattie cut up vegetables for a Mexican-style omelet, dicing Ortega chili peppers, onions, and tomatoes into little chunks. Her grandfather had gone out in his dented, rusting pickup truck to inform Ned, their foreman, about the intruder. Months ago a crew had removed the brown bags covering the date trees, along with the delicate fruit, and now Ned was pruning them with the help of a small crew of men. It could even have been one of them, Margo told herself.

In unusually good spirits, Hattie sang an old Irish tune her mother had taught her. "*In Dublin's fair city, where the girls are so pretty . . .*" All at once she stopped to check the timer on the oven, having slipped in a double batch of chocolate chip cookies earlier.

The rich aroma caused little hungry rumblings in Margo's stomach. "Those cookies smell wonderful, Hattie." Margo adjusted the suede vest she was wearing and smoothed down the colorful feathers and Indian beads.

"I must taste one before I leave," Julie said. She had put the white linen dress back on.

Hattie ignored her. "Margo, when those cookies cool down I want you to take them over to the Circle G Ranch, along with our thanks. And make sure the foreman gets his share."

Margo pursed her lips. "No way."

Hattie's brows drew together, and something slid out of her hand.

The idea of taking cookies to Rebel and Ed sounded terribly old-fashioned, Margo thought. She shook her head at Julie when Hattie leaned down to pick up a piece of onion off the floor. Julie rolled her eyes and looked up at the ceiling.

Hattie straightened and lobbed a piercing stare at her niece. "Something wrong with that, missy?"

Margo cleared her throat. "It's just that I've got so much to do today. I—"

"Nonsense! You've got plenty of time to run these over after Julie leaves. I like Rebel. He's a decent sort of man, the kind that likes to give bear-hugs. I bet he likes kids I might add, his foreman is a swell fella as well. And what a talker!"

Margo hadn't confided to her aunt what she'd over-heard at Rebel's, thinking it wise to find out more first. She turned to her friend. "Could you drop the cookies off on your way home, Julie?"

Julie was about to reply when Hattie cut in, scowling. "You'll take them, Missy!"

Margo knew her aunt well enough to know when she'd been bested. She sighed. "If you insist."

Hattie scooped the vegetables off the cutting board and dropped them into a sizzling, shiny copper skillet, along with the mixture of eggs. The kitchen filled with the tantalizing fragrance of the bubbling omelet.

She seemed preoccupied. No longer frowning, she ex-pertly flipped the omelet over. Margo wondered if the cookie idea wasn't concocted for the pure purpose of impressing Rebel's foreman, Ed. She hid a smile behind her hand. Her aunt was wearing lipstick, something she usually reserved for special occasions.

Julie slipped her shapely figure into a chair at the table. "Now that Rebel's given a party, you ought to be neighborly and do the same—inviting me, of course." The corners of her mouth turned up. "Michael plays golf with him, and he says he's about thirty-five. But he didn't have much else to say. Probably jealous."

Margo grinned in spite of herself. "Don't you think that giving a party would be a little obvious?"

Julie frowned. "Obvious? Why do you say that?"

Hattie spoke up. "Wait a minute." She smoothed back her graying hair, a twinkle in her hazel eyes. "I don't see what's so wrong with Julie's notion."

Margo shook her head. "You're kidding? You know

Grandpa would never go for that." She could just imagine the scene he would make if a Gentry set foot on their property. Since losing his wife, he saw only the dark side of things.

"We need to be thinking about the ranch, not giving parties," she said curtly. "If we could only get a good price for the alfalfa crop. But it's no longer in demand like it used to be. Less horses and cattle—more tract houses. Ugh!"

Hattie looked disappointed. She cut the omelet into three sections and slipped the portions onto warmed plates, handing them to Margo and Julie. "Have a piece of my walnut coffeecake too."

Julie took a square, a twinkle in her eyes. "You like Ed Granger, then?" she said to Hattie.

"The man's got a sense of humor. Kept me in stitches all evening." She chuckled, shaking her head.

Margo took a sip of steaming coffee, smiling over the rim at her aunt. "I'm sure your homemade cookies will be thanks enough."

Hattie's mouth drooped. She picked at the omelet. "I think I'll take the cookies over on my way to Mass, after all, if you're so blamed busy." Her words sounded angry but Margo saw her eyes soften.

"I really need to take Rouge for a workout, that's all," she countered.

Somehow, the thought of seeing Rebel left her giddy. His rugged good looks and proprietary way, confused her. Better to stay far away from him. Then she remembered the auction and her promise. Maybe she could get out of it.

Hattie turned to Julie. "Why don't you go riding with

Margo this morning? You can use my horse. Margo's been on me to exercise Merrybelle more."

"Horse people!" Julie chuckled. "You know horses and I were never on friendly terms. Besides, I've got a lunch date." She bit into the coffeecake.

"Don't tell me—Michael Jonson?" Margo asked.

Her friend dabbed at the corners of her mouth with a paper napkin. "Mind reader! Don't you think he's wonderful? Honestly, I had no idea he'd be at the barbecue!"

Margo frowned. "Is it really wise to get involved with your boss? You know what they say about office romances."

Julie coiled a strand of hair around her finger. "There's nothing serious between us. He simply wants to explain a new project he has in the works."

Margo rose with a noncommittal shrug and put her dishes in the sink. Giving Julie and her aunt a little wave, she pushed open the screen door. "See you later, gals."

Margo opened the stall gate and led Rouge out, giving the mare a carrot to munch while she saddled her. The morning was quiet, with only a light breeze stirring the old windmill near the barn. Yet somehow apprehension dogged her because of the intruder, causing her to glance in dim corners. The sheriff might not think it was a big deal, but it left her feeling wary, and she didn't like that.

Rouge nickered softly. Margo mounted the gentle mare and headed her toward the purple flowering alfalfa fields next to the date grove. She breathed in the pungent scent. Rouge leaned her long, graceful neck down to nip the head off of the first healthy green plant they came to.

"Dessert, huh," Margo said to the horse, laughing.

The azure sky stretched like a giant umbrella, encompassing the San Jacinto peak to the west and the rising Santa Rosa mountains to the south. Whipped-cream clouds hovered over tall pines far up on the mountainside. She swayed to the rhythm of Rouge's slow gait as they moved down the rows.

Riding always relieved Margo's pent-up stress. She might be worried about her grandfather or how they were going to pay the taxes, but not out here. Her expeditions had the effect of giving her a feeling of oneness with nature. She loved the outdoors and the silence broken only by birds and scampering wildlife.

Once through the fields, Margo put Rouge into a canter and headed toward the open desert. The mare's hooves dug into the earth as she plunged ahead. White sand, dappled with lavender verbena, rolled out like a carpet extending all the way to the stark foothills. A hawk circled lazily above a sun-seared canyon. The wet spring had produced a profusion of colorful wildflowers. The beauty of the landscape left Margo spellbound. It always had. The desert was as subtly beautiful as any Renoir painting she'd seen in a book.

Margo reached the border of Desert Jade property and turned into a dry wash. Indolent in the saddle, she rode on, letting the sun warm her bare arms. Then, without warning, Rouge came to an abrupt halt, almost unseating Margo. The distinct rattle and hiss of a rattlesnake pierced the solitude. Rouge tossed her head, whipped her mane, and whinnied in terror.

Alert to danger, Margo glanced down. The snake lay coiled in the horse's path, its rattlers singing a menacing song of doom. A few feet farther and Rouge's legs would have been enmeshed with the deadly creature, along with Margo's ankles. Shuddering, she yanked back on the reins but the mare didn't respond.

Why hadn't Margo thought to bring along her .22? Rouge stamped her hooves and reared back in fearful agitation while Margo clung to the pommel. The snake struck but missed, then curled again—readying.

"Whoa, girl! Settle down!" Margo cried out, trying to gain control.

She ran a hand over Rouge's neck and held the reins securely as the horse fidgeted.

Just then rifle fire broke the stillness with an alarming roar. Rouge lunged sideways. The snake jumped a foot, then fell, writhing into a dying coil. Margo swiveled her head around as the horse whirled.

"Didn't mean to scare you," Rebel drawled from up on the bank, replacing his rifle in its sheath on the saddle. His horse blew threw its nose. "What are you doing out this way?" He eyed Margo with a curious grin spreading across his bronzed, unshaven face.

"I—I could ask you the same thing," she said bluntly.

Watching her, he cleared his throat. "Just checking my borders. Then I saw a rider. Didn't realize it was our fair lady vet." He swung his gaze toward the vineyard, then back to her. "This is Circle G property, ma'am."

"Your land? I didn't realize anyone owned it. Pardon me for trespassing." Margo knew her embarrassment must show in the heating of her cheeks.

"Believe me, you're pardoned." He smiled as his horse pawed the earth. "I bought it about six months ago. Guess you haven't heard. Be my guest anytime, though. We don't shoot trespassers. In fact, if you'll allow me, I'll ride along. Where are you heading?"

"Nowhere in particular—just giving Rouge a workout. It's peaceful out here," she said, her nerves quieting a little. "That is, until that blamed snake showed up. By the way, thanks. You're a good shot."

He fixed Margo with a satisfied grin. The thought occurred to her that he might have followed her. But she didn't want to think so and dismissed the idea. The scratches on the backs of his hands showed plainly he wasn't a gentleman farmer. Besides, he wouldn't have time to do anything so unproductive.

She threw him a rueful smile, trying to sound completely calm when she was anything but inside. "I think I had my horse pretty well under control—until you shot that rifle."

"Didn't mean to spook the mare." He headed his buckskin gelding at an angle down the side of the wash, drawing up to her. "I come this way sometimes when I'm trying to figure out what to do with this fool land now that I own it. Michael Jonson sold it to me. He's a real snake-oil salesman." He laughed. "This land is so full of prairie-dog holes I doubt if I could ever get a vine to take hold."

Margo agreed. "I'm sorry if I sounded ungrateful. I should have been more observant. Those scaly things give me the willies."

"Have to agree with you there. Let's get out of this wash before we find the rest of its cousins and uncles and aunts. I'll show you where my property ends up in the canyon, if you're game."

The gelding swished his long tail at a horsefly. "So?" Rebel said, waiting.

Margo swallowed hard, torn between curiosity and the need to be alone, but she finally nodded. "Sure, I'd like to see it. Before long there won't be any open spaces left. The valley has already been irreversibly altered by all the development. I guess I sound selfish, wanting to keep this land the way it formerly was, but that's how I feel."

Rebel frowned. "No," he said, sympathetic. "But that's progress for you." He lowered the brim of his cowboy hat as his horse carefully skirted the snake. "Let's head out this way."

Rouge stepped lively, obviously glad to escape the presence of the snake.

"I have a recurring dream," Margo said, looking up toward the foothills. She let her gaze sweep back down into the valley behind them, hesitating to go on.

"Oh? What is it?" he prompted.

She leveled on him, not smiling. "A terrible sandstorm comes up and destroys all the tracts here in the desert, leveling the malls, houses, and condominiums— blowing them right out of the valley. Then, when the wind settles down, everything looks pristine."

"Wow! What a diabolic imagination you've got, Doc! I hope you never have a reason to get mad at me." He chuckle. "But isn't that just wishful thinking?"

"I suppose it's my subconscious working overtime." She didn't comment on having a probable reason to be mad at him.

Margo rode alongside the big buckskin, furtively studying Rebel's strong, angular profile. He took no notice. She admired his easy style of riding, like a man born to the saddle.

He pointed toward a billowing cloud formation in the northern sky. "Looks like a giant mountain goat."

"Hmm. Are we looking at the same thing? Frankly, I think it could be a bale of cotton."

He grinned.

She eyed him closely. "Sounds like we're playing a Rorschach game. You into psychology or something?"

"I took a turn on the couch once. But it wasn't my thing."

Margo laughed lightly, feeling a little less unstrung in his presence. She knew so little about him.

Rebel turned in the saddle to face her full on. He had a way of letting his gaze travel over her, unraveling her nerves. She glanced away. "I'm glad you came the other night," he said.

She nodded a thanks.

They let the horses set their own pace, the reins slack on their smoothly elegant necks. When they reached the slope of the foothills leading into the canyons, Rebel drew in the gelding. "This is it," he said proudly. "My land goes right up into those hidden canyons."

Margo glanced around. "I'm afraid you can't plant anything here." She chuckled, hoping he didn't take offense. "A flash flood would wash everything away in a matter of minutes. But maybe you could rent it out to some company wanting to make a western movie."

She turned back to view the picturesque valley sprawling below them. Except for the tracts, it could have been a slice of Egypt, if she didn't know better.

"Oh well, it was just an idea," he said. "Seriously, my intention has always been to keep this area virgin territory. I take it that meets with your approval."

"Absolutely!"

Margo jumped down from the saddle to stretch. She didn't want to believe Rebel, or one of the others for that matter, might have sent the intruder to the Fitzgerald ranch last night. But that's what Grandpa Fitz believed. In the light of day it seemed preposterous. She tethered Rouge to an ironwood bush. Rebel heaved himself out of the saddle, dropped his horse's reins in the sand, and shielded his eyes. He scanned his ranch as though he were seeing it for the first time.

"Look, I've located my house over that sand dune," he said. "Seems like every time I ride up here I get a sense of being at the edge of the world. Its stillness and beauty take my breath away." He looked a little embarrassed by his emotional revelation.

Margo could only agree. "I love the valley, but seeing it slowly slide into the hands of developers like Jonson Enterprises, with their eagerness for a quick buck, breaks my heart. I know Michael's your friend, but . . ."

Rebel didn't comment and she felt disinclined to finish the sentence.

Glowing in the noon sun, beyond the towns, the valley's miles of velvety alfalfa fields, citrus, date groves, and white sand dunes, seemed like her bit of paradise. She was beginning to believe it might even be Rebel's.

He took off his hat and combed his fingers through his thick, dark hair. Perspiration beaded on his forehead from the heat. "Coming up here is like putting the world on hold for a little while."

She glanced back into the canyon. "We haven't seen any bighorn sheep today, but I spotted tracks over toward that mesquite bush."

With his interest still in the landscape, Rebel said, "That must be your reservoir down there to the right."

"Why, yes, it is," she said. Cream-colored sand circled a small sapphire lake.

"The weather's hot enough for a swim. I don't suppose you'd consider letting me take a dip there sometime?"

Astonished, she said, "You have a pool, don't you?"

"But yours looks more inviting."

"Sure, anytime. Seriously, when I was a kid, before my folks were killed, I used to look forward to spending every summer's day there. I lived in town with my parents then." She took off her hat and dropped down on the sand, folding her jeans-clad legs up under her chin. Rebel lowered himself down beside her.

"What happened to them, if you don't mind my asking?"

"They died in a plane crash coming through the San Gorgonio Pass into Palm Springs."

"I'm sorry. My father's still alive and doing well, but my mother passed away too." He didn't tell her about his young, self-possessed stepmother, nor his mistake in picking a fiancée too similar to her. He gazed at Margo's open face, and something stirred in his blood.

"I'm sorry you lost your mom." She patted his hand sympathetically.

Before he realized what he was doing, he leaned over and brushed her lips with his without attempting to embrace her. Her eyes flew open.

"Sorry, I just had to do that," he said, his voice husky. He didn't apologize further or ask if she minded.

A corner of her mouth twitched. "I wasn't expecting that."

"Didn't mean to startle you. It's just that I find you very attractive," he said.

Margo blinked. "Thanks for the compliment, but do you always go around kissing women you find attractive?"

"The kiss only means something if you want it to." His hand covered hers and he gently added pressure.

She straightened, drawing it away, and looked at him levely. "Rebel, I hardly know you." There was a catch in her throat. "And I must admit, I have a lot of questions."

"Like?"

"All right. Here goes." She told him what she had overheard.

Although surprised, Rebel didn't hesitate. "What we were discussing has nothing to do with your ranch, Margo. I'm sorry you got the wrong impression. Michael brought the three of us together for a business deal some time back, although I almost wish he hadn't now. The parcel of land in question is an orange grove near the La Quinta Country Club, and the title is clouded. That's about it. Okay?"

Margo's heart felt lighter, even if she wasn't quite convinced. "You did make us that offer."

"Is that a crime?"

"No, of course it isn't. And I never meant to eavesdrop."

"Things like that can happen."

"Yes, things like that can." Her reply had a double edge.

Rebel leaned over and framed her face with his hands. "I can't honestly say if Huntington and Michael might be up to something I don't know about. But if either of them tried, they'd have to answer to me." He examined her reaction closely. "You're awfully pretty, Dr. Margo

Fitzgerald, and I want to get to know you better—much better—if you'll let me."

Margo pulled away and got to her feet. "I'll have to think about that," she said.

A part of her didn't want to get too involved with Rebel, even though she was attracted by his strong masculinity and the passion barely hidden in his eyes. Yet another part of her remained cautious. How did she know whether he was telling the truth?

"I didn't bring you here to take advantage of you," he said hoarsely, stepping back. His mouth twisted into an apologetic smile. "Guess I'm not any good at trying to be subtle."

She didn't let her eyes waver. "In all honesty I didn't try to stop you."

He grinned. "Yeah, I noticed."

She took a deep, calming breath and exhaled. "We ought to be going."

He picked up his hat and dusted it off on his muscular thigh.

She wanted to know a great deal more but thought better about asking at that moment. Undoubtedly a powerful man, Rebel was used to getting his way. He had been a New York lawyer and had transitioned himself into a successful rancher in no time. His vineyards were the biggest in the valley.

She admired strong men, yet feared them too. They could so easily dominate their women. Her grandfather was a perfect example. She didn't know if Rebel Gentry had a dark side. And what if his kiss was some sort of test? Maybe he thought she just liked a good time. The idea sent her hustling to her horse.

"I just remembered something," she stammered,

swinging into the saddle. "Kane invited me to his polo game and I'm probably going to be late." She adjusted her boots in the stirrups and glanced back at him. "It's been nice seeing you again."

Rebel stood there a moment, hands on hips, his dusky brows furrowing together like an eagle's. "Kane!" he muttered with obvious disapproval. Sighing heavily, he took up the reins and hefted himself into the saddle. "Oh, by the way," he called, changing the subject, "did you find out if you can go to the auction?"

Margo nodded. "I'll work it in."

"Great! I'll call you and set up a time."

Chapter Six

When Margo arrived back at the Desert Jade, she unsaddled Rouge and brushed her down with a curry-comb. Then she led the mare back into the stall and filled up the trough with plenty of fresh water. Horsehair had collected on her jeans. She brushed at it, wishing she could brush away her feelings for the Southerner just as easily.

Margo came into the kitchen. Hattie was humming. She looked up from where she was pulling apart lettuce leaves at the kitchen sink and smiled warmly. "Lunch is almost ready, hon. Have a nice ride, did you?"

Margo returned her aunt's smile. "Yes, I did." She poured a glass of water. Hattie's expectant gaze asked more than whether Margo had had a nice horseback ride, but she let it drop.

"Did you see Ed Granger this morning?" Margo asked, setting the glass on the counter too hard. It made a cracking noise. She picked it up and examined the bottom. "You seem so upbeat. Could a little romance be brewing?"

"Poppycock!" Hattie snorted, her demeanor changing. "Where do you get such notions?"

"You said he was awfully nice," she reminded her aunt, placing the glass back on the counter with more care.

"Yes, he is. But don't go around building mountains out of molehills." Hattie tossed the lettuce into a wooden bowl and dried her hands on the apron she wore.

"By the way, did you see Rebel when you were over at his ranch this morning?" Curious, Margo couldn't keep herself from asking.

"Aren't you full of questions? Yeah, but just for a minute or two. He said he was going to ride his horse out to the back vineyards. Ed told me his boss works like a mule right alongside his men. Before I left I told Rebel he ought to catch up with you."

Margo perched on the edge of a kitchen chair, tugging at a boot. It accidentally flew out of her hands, thumping on the floor.

"Butterfingers!" Hattie exclaimed. "First the glass and now your boot. What's with you, child?"

Margo grinned sheepishly, ignoring the implication. "Did you tell him where I planned to ride?"

"No. How would I know? And why are you giving me the third degree? I bet you saw him. That's it, right?"

"Ah . . . yes," Margo said, breaking into a grin. So he had followed her after all. Her heart beat faster. She ought to be furious, but somehow she wasn't.

"You didn't mention it when you came in," Hattie said. "You're so secretive."

Her aunt's mouth was forming around another question when Margo abruptly glanced at the clock over the refrigerator.

"It's late. I'm going to the polo field. Kane invited me."

"Hmm. That Jonson fella called." Hattie raised her eyes. "Good thing Daddy didn't take the message. He thinks the man's the devil incarnate." She took a slip of paper from her apron pocket and handed it over.

"What's he want?" Margo barely took time to glance at the number. "Did he say?"

"Not to me. More than likely he wants this ranch. What else?"

"I'll call when I get around to it—maybe." She didn't think much of Michael. He and Julie were probably already on the verge of having a romance. "I've got to change my clothes. See you later, Hattie," she called over her shoulder, as she hurried down the hall to her bedroom.

Margo removed her clothes and tossed them in the hamper, then peered at her face in the bathroom mirror. She ran a finger lightly over her lower lip, trying to recapture the lovely sensation of Rebel's kiss. But the feeling was lost. Sighing, she slipped into white slacks, a royal blue blouse, and a sun hat, and left the house.

She wheeled down the country lane past Rebel's vineyards. The more she was around him, the more interesting he became—and mysterious. Kane, on the other hand, might be the handsomest man she had ever met but he bored her. He was undoubtedly used to women fawning all over him too. Should she be speeding along, acting like just another groupie? The mere thought caused her to ease her foot off the gas pedal and consider making a U-turn in the middle of the road. But her curiosity got the better of her. After all, she wasn't marrying him.

The parking lot was nearly full. She found a space in the shade of a tamarack tree and got out. The loud grunts of men and horses told her the game must be in full swing.

Inside the grounds fans wearing hats and sunglasses perched on bleachers. She located a place to sit and quickly became absorbed in the action.

Long-legged, agile Thoroughbreds dashed madly up and down the field, making perilous turns while their riders swatted a plastic ball with mallets. Kane, dressed in a helmet and white jodhpurs, bent low to exercise a particularly difficult maneuver between two charging horses. Everyone applauded when he succeeded, including Margo.

During a break in the game, he swung out of the saddle, his face flushed, his clothes spattered with dirt. A groom led his tired horse away and brought out a fresh animal. Then Kane, along with the other players, mounted and leaped back into the fray, attempting to drive the ball through the opposing team's goal. Margo admired his skill, the way he used the mallet without it getting tangled up in a horse's legs.

The opposing team suddenly pulled ahead and the tension mounted. She could hardly sit still. But Kane's team racked up three goals in quick succession to win. She stood up and cheered with the fans. Kane jumped down from his mount and glanced around, pushing back his helmet.

Margo called out. "Kane!"

He turned when he saw her coming toward him across the churned-up grass and smiled broadly, holding up his dirt-encrusted arms in the victory sign. This man was a boy at heart.

"Ah, Margo, darling! Glad you could make it. Let me get out of these clothes and I'll meet you in the clubhouse for refreshments. Great afternoon!" For once he didn't make some sort of smart remark.

"You were very good," she said. "I can see you're quite experienced in the saddle."

He grinned, running his glove across his brow, spreading some of the dirt. "And elsewhere too." He took off his helmet and his light hair lay plastered to his scalp. Rivulets of perspiration cascaded down his cheeks. "You look absolutely beautiful underneath your sun hat—cool too," he said. "Blasted heat!"

Margo smiled. "Thanks." She suspected he was used to dishing out compliments and had already made up her mind not to take anything he said seriously. But she was flattered all the same. It would be easy for a woman to surrender to a charismatic man like Kane.

He tugged at the horse's reins, and the tired Thoroughbred patiently followed him off the field. Margo headed for the small clubhouse, taking her time as she mentally examined a golden horse still on the field. She had treated it recently for a knee joint problem. The Arabian looked in good shape after the arduous workout. She didn't see Phar, however. It would be another week or two before he'd be fit for the next meet.

Players gathered in the clubhouse, losers congratulating winners. Kane sauntered through the door in a little while and she waved him over. He looked dapper in white slacks and a navy blue golf shirt.

"Hi," he said, pointing to her drink. "Another?"

"Thanks. Mineral water."

A short, stocky man in his forties came over and slapped Kane on the back.

"Great game, old fellow!"

Kane gave him a mock slug on the arm, and they laughed heartily like old comrades. "You'll have me out of the saddle and flat on my back next time," Kane said, taking a gulp of his drink.

The man chuckled. "You never know, do you?" Then he turned away, nodding politely to Margo.

Kane threw his leg over the back of the chair and sat down beside Margo, showing no signs of being weary from the game. "That guy fell off his horse in the first period." He snickered in a low voice and motioned to the man's back.

She thought about the horse trainers and owners she had worked with at the racetrack. "You men are so competitive. Sometimes I think you view life as one big game."

He laughed. "You could be right."

"I used to be a track vet," she said, "before coming home to live."

"Really? Sounds extraordinary, you being a woman. What made you give it up?"

"I reached the point where I couldn't put another injured racehorse out of its misery. A lot of them shouldn't be running in the first place. I never liked prescribing Lasix to horses whose lungs bleed during a race, either. If they can't run without bleeding, well then, I think it's wrong to race them. But I suppose you didn't invite me here for a lecture. I must be boring you silly."

"Not at all. Go on."

"No, that's enough pontificating." She threw him an easy smile.

"Ready, then?" He gulped his drink down.

Margo nodded, wishing she hadn't gotten so serious, but sometimes the old memories came back to trouble her.

Kane's black Ferrari was parked at the opposite end of the field from her car. He swung the door open for her, then jogged around and got behind the wheel. She ran her palm over the expensive leather seat, appreciating its glove like softness, and leaned back to fasten the seatbet. Kane didn't bother to buckle up.

He whipped the car out of the parking lot and raced down the avenue. Margo held her breath as he accelerated. Clearly he drove like he rode horses.

When they passed by the Circle G's vineyards, she glanced toward a sea of green vines and thought she caught a glimpse of Rebel working among the men.

They covered the twenty-five miles to the Salton Sea in breathtaking time. He squealed into a parking lot, the Ferrari's tires crunching over gravel. Margo's knees felt like sponges when she got out. They entered the semi-dark interior of the drab seaside diner. Kane found them a booth near a window. She slid in, wishing the grimy booth were cleaner. Instead of taking the seat opposite, he moved cozily in beside her. In the back of her mind, she wished Rebel were with her instead of Kane. But this was to be a spying expedition to find out just what Kane might know.

A blond waitress with a skirt about as long as the tail on Margo's blouse, sashayed up to them and threw Kane a familiar smile.

"Hi, Dolly." He grinned.

"You're back, darlin'," she said, chewing her gum with the intensity of a piranha.

"Bring us two coffees," he replied.

Margo resented his ordering for her. Coffee would not have been her choice. She glanced around, surprised Kane would frequent such a place. It lacked the sophistication she thought he'd demand. The roadhouse did have an excellent view of the majestic Salton Sea and the lavender-tinted mountain range jutting up behind it like one of Gauguin's backdrops. The sun had already begun its descent, and peach-colored beams cast golden shimmers over the sparkling azure water.

"I like this place," Kane said. "It's funky and off the beaten track. And it's old and musty, like a real English pub. I enjoy looking out there and seeing the water too. It's a strange lake—full of salt, but then you already know about that."

Margo nodded. She looked away and thought she saw Rebel's Range Rover speed by on the highway. But he wouldn't be out this way, would he? The waitress returned with the coffee and a basket of tortilla chips.

Kane seemed to relish the coffee, not noticing that Margo barely sipped hers.

Margo asked, "Aren't you getting hungry? Maybe we should eat now."

He ignored her question. "So you like polo?"

She nodded. "The horses are splendid."

"The challenge is what tempts me. Who doesn't like to win? I'd show you my trophies, but they're back in the U.K." He put down his cup. "Like to see them? How about right now? We'll fly over tonight." He stood and took her arm as though to leave, but Margo pulled it away, nearly choking on his outlandish suggestion.

"Not tonight, Kane," she managed to say in a neutral tone, as though he had asked her to go to a movie.

He looked slightly baffled by her failure to respond to him. He gulped the remains of the coffee and ordered another round, even though Margo held up her hand and said "No." She hadn't finished the first one.

His chin pulled down in disappointment, but his arm slid around the padded back of her seat, and his fingers caressed her collarbone. Margo moved slightly forward, displacing his fingers, giving him a displeased look. Her frustration level climbed and she asked herself, What am I doing here?

"I wanted to ask you about your father's offer," she said, trying for an opening before the man was off and talking about himself again.

Kane laughed. "You know he wants your ranch, Margo. Why don't you break down and sell it? He'll give you a better price than Jonson Enterprises, or Rebel Gentry, for that matter. They're a couple of tightwads, my father says."

So they had discussed it with him. "It's not for sale," she snapped, "and never will be. Is that why you asked me out, to make this proposition?" He must be as underhanded as she herself.

He studied her, his eyes unreadable, and took out a cigarette. "That's not the proposition I had in mind, dear lady."

Normally Margo was a peaceful, nonviolent person, but by now she had had enough of Kane Huntington and would have liked to smack him and go home.

"Let's order dinner now," she demanded frostily. This had been a bad idea from the get-go. The swirl of his cigarette smoke burned her eyes.

"Excuse my bad manners," he said. "It's so early, but

if you're hungry, why, we'll order everything on the menu. Ha-ha."

"I don't think that's necessary." She tried to be pleasant. "A sandwich will do."

"Dolly!" he boomed to the waitress who stood talking to a cowboy-type across the room at the high bar. She was resting her elbow on the counter and her knee triangulated out. "Get over here. This lady wants dinner."

The waitress wriggled over with menus, her mouth in a bow. "I know what you want, handsome. Always the same—chili with extra soda crackers. If it weren't for your accent, I'd take you for a Texan."

Kane heehawed. Margo ordered chili too, making a silent decision to leave, one way or the other, after they had eaten. She could always call Julie to come and get her. The waitress headed for the kitchen. Suddenly, Kane's hand veered under the table and landed on her knee. Flinching, Margo shook off his paw. But he quickly planted it there again and gave her a wet kiss on the cheek. "I like you," he breathed in a husky voice.

"Stop it," she growled, inching away from him and flinging his hand from her as though it were a dead fish. "You're overstepping the boundaries."

Kane shrugged, and lit another cigarette. Without warning, he dropped it in the ashtray and reached over, taking Margo in his arms. He smothered her lips in a kiss that tasted of stale tobacco. She struggled free and threw him a withering glance.

"Stop it, you idiot! Keep you hands off me!" She pushed him so hard he landed on the floor with a thump. She slid off the seat, grabbed her purse, and looked for a telephone booth. Patrons swiveled their heads, warm glints of amusement lighting their faces at her outrage.

She spun around and started across the floor, nearly careening into a tall man who had just come in. His big flame was outlined by the outdoor floodlights. His gaze swung meaningfully to her.

"Rebel?" she whispered. Surely he hadn't followed her, but she hoped with all her heart he had this time.

"Margo?"

She cleared her throat, straightening. His appearance had to be more than a coincidence but at this point she didn't care.

He took one look at Kane, who'd just regained his footing. "Need a lift home, Margo?"

"You'll never know how much."

She glared at the polo player over her shoulder as he shakily sat down.

"Kane, slide yourself out of there," Rebel said with a menacing straightening of his shoulders.

His eyes were as grimly cold as the inside of a frozen turkey and he'd doubled his fists. Margo stood behind him, peering around his bent elbow.

The smile Kane summoned up was sickly pale, making her want to chuckle.

"Just a minute," he said, ready to argue. "I don't like your tone. I—"

"Now!"

Grumbling, Kane stood up. Rebel didn't hit him but gave the polo player a shove that sent him reeling backward across the floor to the bar. The waitress and the cowboy jumped out of the way. Then Rebel took Margo's hand and marched her toward the door to his Range Rover. She felt like a little girl being escorted by her daddy.

As she and Rebel drove out of the dark parking lot,

she asked, "How did you happen to come to this place at precisely the same time Kane and I were here?"

He didn't answer right away, but seemed to give it some thought, his jaw muscle working. "Is there a law against it? The tavern is a popular watering hole around here."

"Oh. I know I must sound like a shrew but I'm grateful all the same. I didn't think he'd behave like that."

He coughed. "It appeared you needed a helping hand."

Unable to resist, she asked again, "Did you follow us?"

He gave her an irritating, sidelong glance. "Don't flatter yourself."

"If you didn't, then how else would you know I was there?"

"Give it a rest."

She clasped her hands in her lap and dug her nails into her flesh, not liking his impertinent answer. Then she remembered. "My Cherokee's at the polo field. Would you mind dropping me off there?"

"No problem."

They rode to the polo field in dead silence. Margo vacillated between wanting to thank him again for saving her from the date-from-Hades and continuing to accuse him.

Chapter Seven

The following day, a dozen red roses arrived at the veterinary clinic for Margo. Kane had included a mushy note. She tore it into tiny pieces, then tossed the flowers and note into a wastebasket. But Grace, the receptionist, retrieved the roses as soon as Margo left the room and placed them in a vase on her own desk.

Rebel brought his hound in for an eye examination in the afternoon. Margo put on her "vet" manners, attempting to treat him as just another worried owner.

"If you hadn't called my attention to this ol' boy's condition at the barbecue," he said, "I guess I wouldn't have noticed until it got worse." He rubbed the dog's chest with his splayed palm.

Margo handed him a tube of ointment. "He'll be fine now. Just put a little of this in his eyes, morning and night. He's in pretty good shape, considering his age."

Rebel had lifted the dog to a metal examining table and now he looked across the dog's back at her. "Thanks, Margo." He hesitated, as though he wanted to say more, then helped the dog down.

"You're welcome," she said, disappointed.

She handed him the leash and watched him stroll out of the room with the dog.

Then he turned back briefly. "Don't forget the auction, okay?"

She nodded, not wanting him to see her pleasure.

On Saturday, Rebel drove up to the Desert Jade entrance. Margo stood by the rural mailbox. Since she hadn't been to an auction in a long time, she looked forward to the excitement of seeing the horses parade around the arena. Interested buyers would bid on them.

Driving away, he said, "I'm counting on you to find me a good gelding."

His Stetson lay on the backseat, the low crown indented just right on the sides.

"I hope there'll be a large selection," Margo replied. She sat back, delighted to be out in the early spring afternoon. "But I'm sure you already know the difference between cabbages and kings. You won't have any difficulty picking out a fine horse yourself."

"That's where you're wrong. We had horses on the plantation when I was a kid, but I went away to boarding school early on. After that I'd ride when I came home, but it wasn't the same as being around them enough to know what makes a sound horse and what doesn't."

"At these auctions you never know whether sellers will haul out some fine bloodlines or a bunch of old nags." Margo smiled. "But I can advise you on any health problems I might see."

She still doubted Rebel needed her expertise, as she doubted many things about him. Yet his nearness stirred something inside her as she watched his strong hands grasp the steering wheel. She recalled how he had handled Kane so easily, his energy alone a threat. Contrary to what he said, he must have been standing there observing them for some time.

Rebel felt her eyes on him and turned briefly to slant a smile her way. From the first time he'd laid eyes on her he had been attracted. The thought caused a pleasurable fire to simmer through him.

"Looks like a good day for an auction," she said, bringing him back to reality.

"Yeah, I'm looking forward to it."

Rebel tried to make light conversation but knew he didn't have the gift for gab that someone like Kane Huntington had. However, after Kane got too familiar and made a fool of himself, he was quite sure Margo wasn't gaga over the guy—if she ever had been. He swallowed hard, just thinking about it. Sometimes Rebel had a hard time articulating his feelings, and Roxanne Humphreys, his former fiancée, had accused him of being remote. But that was hogwash. He glanced over at Margo and grinned. She inclined her head. He tried to keep his eyes on the road.

Margo was so different from the women he grew up with. While Southern women tried to get their way by skirting around an issue, Margo went straight to the point and held her ground. She seemed unaware of her attractiveness, not trying to use it to advantage the way Roxanne had done. But that was a closed chapter in his life.

The ginger color of Margo's hair, neatly done up in a French braid, definitely didn't come out of a bottle, he figured. Character and passion mingled in her unusual eyes. The simple blue jeans and crisp plaid western shirt she wore looked terrific on her. He noticed she had shined her boots. For him maybe?

Her full lips were provocatively tempting when she said, "We're almost there."

He didn't detect any sign of makeup, other than a light touch of lipstick. Margo Fitzgerald was beguilingly unaffected and a natural beauty.

They reached the rutted road leading into the dusty auction grounds and found a parking place among Suburbans, Jeeps, pickups, campers, and various horse trailers.

"So this is where the auctions are held," he said, grabbing his hat as they got out.

"It used to be a stud farm."

The doors of the big, paint-chipped barn lay wide open and people milled around. Margo walked on ahead. Rebel noted the way she moved, the springy lightness of her step. When she glanced around, grinning with joy at being there, it pleased him to see her excitement.

Inside the cavernous barn, Rebel helped Margo climb up the temporary bleachers, admiring her shapely legs. He felt optimistic she'd help him find a suitable horse. The auction was already in progress.

"Look at that one," she said, poking him as a fine black horse high-stepped into view. "You don't see many black stallions in these parts." Her face radiated a keen interest. "But he looks a little spirited for a saddle horse, don't you think?"

Rebel nodded, rejecting it out of hand. The next horse had a bone spavin in its hock joint, where fluid had built up. He was more knowledgeable about horses than he let on. Margo shook her head and turned up her nose.

"I need a calm animal," Rebel reminded her, "a working horse who won't tire of me being in the saddle for long stretches."

"Fortunately, there are lots of horses here today."

Another prancing stallion was brought into the show ring, his head sniffing the air. Margo grinned, shaking her head. "He'd always be looking for a mare, I'm afraid."

Rebel chuckled.

The afternoon unfolded with Margo pointing out bowed legs, split hooves, popped knees, and damaged tendons. Her face glowed in the soft, filtered light inside the barn.

Rebel was beginning to doubt they'd find a horse, when Margo suddenly rose to her feet. "That one!" She pointed, her face lighting up with excitement.

Rebel jumped up too. Taking her word as gospel, he bid on a five-year-old gelding named Jake.

"You won't be sorry," she said when he got the nod of approval from the auctioneer. The horse was now his. "The chestnut's healthy, and he has intelligent eyes. His long legs are plenty strong."

Rebel gave her a little hug and they went down to inspect the horse. She put out her hand to nuzzle the soft hairs above the gelding's upper lip. When she drew away, the horse reached out his elongated face for another rub.

"He wants a carrot," she said. "Too bad I didn't bring one."

"I'll go in and finish the paperwork," Rebel said, leaving her there while he headed for the office.

Margo ran her hands over the horse's flanks. He was part Morgan—wide-chested and powerful.

In the office, Rebel wrote a check and shook hands

with the former owner. Then he called Ed to bring a horse trailer to transport the gelding back to the Circle G. Margo was looking with intense interest at a Tennessee Walker tethered near his new horse when he came back. He'd buy it for her if he thought she wouldn't refuse.

"I think it's about time to celebrate," he said. "What lunch? A new horse? Which one can I buy you first?"

She laughed. "Lunch. And I've already got a horse, although that Tennessee Walker is awfully tempting. I hope your new gelding proves to be just what you need." She patted Jake on the rump and dust swirled. "Better put a groom to work giving him a good bath."

They drove to Palm Desert, a sprawling community near Palm Springs, filled with suntanned vacationers wearing shorts, straw hats, and plenty of sunblock. The restaurant had a brass elephant knocker on the front door and a safari decor interior.

A comely hostess in tan shorts and a safari shirt found them a cozy booth near the patio.

"They have great baby-back ribs and Caesar salads here," Rebel said.

"Good, I'll go for both."

When the waiter came, they ordered. Margo had worked up an appetite.

Rebel's eyes rested on her lower lip, and she fought the compulsion to look away. He caressed the back of her hand, sending tiny sparks of sensation flying up her arm.

"Are you going to rename the horse?" she asked.

"Jake's a good enough name, don't you think?"

"Sure." She liked the timbre of his voice. "Some people spend hours trying to come up with a different handle for a new horse in their stable, but I think that's silly. I wouldn't want my name suddenly changed to Penelope."

Rebel grinned. "I don't imagine horses pay much attention to things like that. But seriously, I think you picked out one fine animal. Glad you came along. Now what can I do to thank you? That Tennessee Walker maybe?"

She laughed. "Not a thing. I hope Jake works out just fine and doesn't come down with some strange malady after I've given him a clean bill of health."

When he shifted, his knee accidentally touched hers. Margo felt the warmth of his body through the soft denim material and hastily drew away, confused by her own attraction to him.

"By the way," she said in a slightly teasing voice, "I would have thought you were raised here in the desert the way you scampered over those boulders the day we rescued Phar."

A grin spread over his bronzed face. "Yeah. I leaped from rock to rock with the grace of a mountain goat."

Margo chuckled. "In truth, I was glad you were in front so you couldn't see my own awkward slips and slides."

He lifted a thick eyebrow. "Wish I could have seen that. I would gladly have lent a hand to such a beautiful lady vet—maybe even picked you up and toted you over my shoulder."

She didn't know whether he was serious or joking, but smiled. He certainly had the broad shoulders to do it.

The waiter brought a tray with a cluster of dishes and they temporarily abandoned conversation. Margo tried to eat the ribs without getting the barbecue sauce on her, but without success. When Rebel leaned over to wipe a smudge of sauce from beside her mouth, she said, "I'm failing miserably again, just as I did at your party. I guess you can't take some people anyplace. But then, you're not having much luck, either. Here . . ." And she wiped away a smudge on his chin.

"Why did I suggest something so messy?" he said.

"No one's looking at us."

"What the heck! These taste too good to worry."

"My feelings exactly. They say a person should only eat ribs and corn-on-the-cob with friends."

He picked up a glass of beer and took a swallow. "Does that mean we're friends?"

His expression looked so hopeful that Margo nodded. "Why, of course."

She leaned back a moment, scrutinizing him openly, letting the corners of her lips turn up. "You remind me of a Black Angus Restaurant commercial I saw on television once—you know, the cowboy cooking over an open fire."

He threw back his head and laughed. "I always wanted to be a cowboy when I was a tyke, but I guess grape ranching here in the desert is as close as I'll come. How about you? Ever want to be anything other than a vet?"

Margo grinned. "Promise you won't laugh?"

He held up his hand, giving her the Scouts' Honor sign. "Promise."

"An opera singer."

"What's so funny about that? I bet you sang solos in your high school chorus."

"Not quite. I mouth the words to hymns in church. Does that tell you anything?"

He rubbed his hands on the napkin. "Tough. Well, you can still sing in the shower, can't you?"

"Ahh, you're right about that—and I do."

The busboy came to take away the dishes. When he left, Rebel asked, "Want another lemonade? Now that I've got you all to myself, I want to keep you here. You're not in a hurry, are you?"

"I've always got loads of things to do, Rebel. But yes, I'll have a glass of lemonade, and thanks." She adjusted her body on the seat, catching the pleasant aroma of his aftershave. "I've had a lovely day."

Rebel extended his arm with a gentle motion and settled it behind her in the booth, not touching her. "We'll have to do this more often."

"Buy another horse?"

He grinned. "No. Go out together. I'm glad you're enjoying yourself. So am I."

His thick eyelashes dropped low over his eyes as he bent to brush her temple with his lips. A tingling sensation remained where his lips had been and her heart fluttered. Yet there was something about him she still didn't quite trust, and it nagged at her.

Raised on a ranch with no brothers didn't make Margo much of a judge of male character. And her controlling grandfather certainly wasn't a good role model, even if he had never been violent. Then the men at the track—well, she wouldn't think about *those* guys. Rebel would probably be amused if he knew how limited was her experience with men. Even though she had dated, she never had a serious relationship. Her self-induced isolation while enrolled in college and veterinary school had helped to place her in the top honors category, yet did nothing for her love life.

At twenty-nine she still considered herself to be a babe in the woods where men were concerned. Sometimes she wished she were more worldly.

The waiter refreshed their beverages. Rebel and Margo sat back, listening to elevator-type music coming over the speakers.

"In truth," he said, "I like elevator music."

Margo chuckled.

His face broke into a wide grin. "You too?"

She nodded in the affirmative.

His fingers drew a gentle line across her shoulders, causing her heart to flutter all over again. She reached for the glass with a trembling hand. "What are your future plans?" she asked, choosing a topic, any topic, to get her mind off his touch. Then she remembered he wanted her ranch.

He puckered his forehead, growing thoughtful. "I want to improve my grapes by infusing them with seedlings from upper California's Napa and Sonoma Valleys. The loam's richer in nutrients up there than here in the desert."

"Yes, taming the desert soil is a lifelong job." Margo gave him an understanding smile. Impulsively Rebel gently squeezed her hand. He wanted to talk of love when all the while they went on discussed these mundane things. But he knew by her gestures and the tone of her voice she wasn't ready for that. However, patience had never been one of his strong suits.

Huntington and Jonson crossed his mind. Surely they weren't up to something devious. Slow to anger, Rebel's rage could be formidable when ignited. Now, the mere thought of one of them causing Margo grief sent an intense fury racing through his limbs. He'd check it out as soon as possible, or his name wasn't Rebel Gentry.

He caught her staring at him and hoped she wasn't reading his thoughts. Her long, golden lashes swept down to close momentarily over her questioning eyes. He traced her cheekbone with his thumb, feeling the soft, silky texture. The act dissolved his immediate anxieties, and he leaned back, more relaxed. "I wanted to do that ever since we met," he said with sincerity.

She sat there as though waiting for him to say something more. Then the waiter appeared at Rebel's elbow with the bill, breaking the spell.

"Anything more, sir?"

Rebel turned to her. "Margo?"

"No, nothing. Thanks. It's getting late and we ought to go."

Rebel paid the bill with a credit card and they left. She didn't say a word about the stolen kiss. He guessed he wasn't in trouble after all. The prospect of stealing another was all too tempting as he slipped an arm around her slim waist and they headed for the Range Rover.

Margo enjoyed his company. She understood that a certain intimacy had developed between them, even if she had no idea where it would lead. The more she was around him, the more she realized the man had depths she could only imagine. And she enjoyed hearing his deep baritone voice rise with enthusiasm when he talked about things that interested him. In truth, she enjoyed the touch of his lips even more.

Outside, a bright canopy of stars sprinkled tiny rhinestones in the sky. They sauntered to his vehicle, his arm still wrapped around her.

"The moon looks as though it might burst into melting gold," Margo said while they stood there a moment.

Rebel nodded and helped her into the vehicle. The courtly gesture amused her. He had all the traits of a Southern gentleman.

He drove her home, taking the long way. When the SUV came to a halt in front of the house, he pulled her into his muscular arms as though he couldn't wait another minute. His gentle kiss was succeeded by another filled with tenderness.

When he let her go, Margo gasped for air. "I don't know what to say, Rebel," she stammered, her lips tingling.

His gaze warmed. "Then don't say anything."

Margo started to open the car door, but his strong grip captured her shoulders. He kissed her again.

Then Margo pulled away. She turned her head before he could kiss her again. "No, Rebel. This is too soon— much too soon."

Reluctantly, he released her, his mouth turning down, his eyes losing the luster that had been there moments before. "Curfew?" he said, giving her a broken grin.

She laughed shakily. "No. Only the one I put on myself."

He reached over to open the door. "When can I see you again?"

"I don't know."

She saw his intense face in the pale light from the domelight overhead and tried to smile through her mixed emotions. Deep down she cared for him more than any man she'd ever met. But she wasn't sure about these wild and threatening inclinations zooming inside her mind.

"How about tomorrow?" he asked. "And the next?"

She didn't reply right away, but hastily reached out to touch his face. The slight roughness of his skin made her catch her breath. This was madness. She hardly knew him.

"I'll call you," he said, as she slid off the seat.

"Yes, I'd like that."

She opened the door with an unsteady hand and threw him a little smile of thanks before closing it after her.

Rebel felt drunk with emotion. He climbed back into the Rover and drove mindlessly toward his ranch. On the way, he rolled down a window and breathed deeply, sucking the fresh night air into his hot lungs in great gulps.

"I probably won't sleep tonight," he growled low in his throat. "This little filly has me lassoed and hog-tied!" He laughed at the old clichés. Yet somehow they fit perfectly. All of a sudden, a bat grazed the windshield and he swerved, whistling in surprise. It brought him back to his senses.

Margo laid awake for hours, trying to make sense of her growing attraction to Rebel Gentry. Outside the window a frog croaked. She had channeled her whole life into her career, and for the first time a man had made her hunger for something more. Working in a man's world, she had ignored her female instincts. And now she found herself listening to her own inner voice. His mere touch caused her to glow and his compliments made her feel beautiful and adored.

She snuggled into the pillow and closed her eyes.

Somewhere off in the distance a coyote gave a mournful wail as though its soulmate had died. A soft breeze rustled through the open shutters, but these familiar things didn't calm her.

Then Margo sat up, sniffing the air. She smelled the distinct odor of burning wood. Fire! Grabbing a robe off the foot of the bed, she dashed out of her room and down the hall, hurriedly checking each room. Nothing. Then, on entering the kitchen, she saw flames licking and sputtering on the roof of a shed outside. In the stables the horses cried out and stamped their hooves. Just then she heard her grandfather's booming voice from behind her.

"Fiiirrre!"

Grandpa Fitz loped through the kitchen and out the backdoor in his nightshirt. Margo, Hattie, and Beauregard, the dog, raced after him. He turned on the garden hose full blast and attempted to douse the orange flames, sending up steamy clouds. The dry old building groaned and hissed, its timbers cracking. The breeze blew embers into the sky like little glowing boats. Margo worried about the stable roof igniting or the house catching on fire.

"They're trying to scare us off!" Grandpa Fitz shouted. He raised his fist in a furious assault on the air."Next it'll be our home!" Clutching his chest, he suddenly fought to get his breath, his face turning beet red. "Get my shotgun. I'll shoot the tail-feathers right off them! Come on out, you varmints. Show yourselves!"

"Calm down, Daddy," Hattie said. "You'll give yourself a heart attack." She put her arm around his rigid shoulders.

"Can't trust anyone at all, at all," he said fervently.

"It's a darn conspiracy. Scare us into selling, will they? Well, it won't work! I'll shoot myself before I'd sell to those tricky thieves!"

Margo shook her head, fearing for his health. "Calm yourself, Grandpa, or it *will* be the death of you." She grabbed his other side. Together she and her aunt got him back into the kitchen. Beauregard whimpered and laid his head across Grandpa Fitz's bare foot.

Hattie put a call in to the sheriff.

Margo filled the kettle and lit a burner under it. "I'll check the horses while you get the tea ready, Hattie. There's not much we can do tonight, except wait for Sheriff Stoney. Grandpa, why don't you go back to bed?"

"I will not!" he said with a firm shake of his head.

She hurried outside, skirted the shed, and made her way to the stables, glancing back apprehensively over her shoulder. The intruder—it had to be the man she saw before—might still be around.

When Margo entered the stables, the horses whinnied as if to say *"Save us."* She peered over Rouge's stall gate, meeting the mare's two enormous, rounded eyes. If the horse had been a cat, she'd have jumped into Margo's lap. Margo rubbed the mare's long nose reassuringly and reached up to stroke her thick mane. Grandpa Fitz's dapple-gray gelding tossed his head in the next stall and nickered. Hattie's horse, Merrybelle, blew nervously out through her nose and took a swipe at the stall wall with her sturdy back legs.

Margo stayed with the horses, calming them until she heard the sound of a car engine coming fast along the road. The sheriff pulled up to the house in his Bronco, his wheels throwing gravel. She rushed out to meet him.

He opened the door and stepped out on the ground. "Got a problem again, Doc?"

"It looks like it." She pointed dismally toward the smoking rubble. At least the embers had subsided.

He took off his hat and ran a hand through his thinning hair, then laid the hat on the hood. "First a prowler, and now a fire. What do you think is coming off here?"

"I wish I knew."

Hattie came outside, looking harried, her hair askance. She had pulled on a shirt and slacks, her shirttail hanging out. Margo glanced down at herself. She was still wearing the terrycloth robe and her feet were bare.

The sheriff sauntered over to where the shed had stood and poked around the hot edges with a stick.

"Someone set that fire, sure as shootin,' " Hattie said. "There wasn't even any electrical wiring inside that shed."

The sheriff coughed. "What did you keep inside there?"

"Not much," Margo said. "It was just a storage shed we used mostly to store equipment at harvest time."

The sheriff glanced around. "Maybe an illegal used it to sleep in and tried to heat up some food. There isn't enough evidence here to do much with, I'm sorry to say, but I smell kerosene."

"Well, come in and have a cup of tea," Hattie said. "No sense our standing out here."

"Can you make it cocoa?"

Hattie nodded, unsmiling.

She seated him at the kitchen table opposite Grandpa, who told him in a loud voice about his conspiracy theory.

Sheriff Stoney said, "Any evidence, sir?"

Grandpa Fitz seemed to crumple in the chair. "No, dang it."

Stoney turned to Margo. "See someone hanging around this time?"

"No, I was in bed. When I smelled smoke, I got up to investigate. The shed was already ablaze."

"Someone's responsible," Hattie insisted bitterly.

"You didn't store paint supplies or old rags in there, did you?"

Margo's nerves were strung taut. "We told you. Never any of that kind of stuff."

Hattie handed Stoney a cup of cocoa and he thanked her. She sat down heavily, staring out the window.

"I'm sorry, folks, but there's nothing much I can do," the sheriff said. He blew on the hot cup and watched a swirl of heat rise.

"Thanks for coming out, anyway," Margo said.

The sheriff finished the mug of cocoa, told them to keep their eyes peeled, and drove away.

Margo still felt jittery. Thankfully, it had only been the shed that burned. It was the kind of dirty trick someone might play to frighten them, but that didn't mean the house wouldn't be next. Grandpa got up and went off to bed, mumbling to himself Beauregard followed at his heels.

"I saw Ed Granger this afternoon," Hattie said, her face softening. "He came by for a cup of coffee. Said he just loved the cookies I baked, and he wants me to go riding with him soon. I just might. Haven't been in the saddle for months. Poor Merrybelle needs a better workout than my making her run around in circles in the paddock."

Margo looked away from the fire's smoking remnants. "I think that's a super idea. Ed seems awfully nice."

"He told me he'd been married. Wife died in childbirth. Isn't that terrible?"

"I can only imagine his grief." Margo thought about her own parents' death, and all of a sudden she was transported back to her childhood, feeling the wrenching emotional pain once again.

"Ed said it tore him up, broke his heart so bad he decided he'd never marry again. But now he's beginning to think differently. Do you suppose that means he's going to ask me to marry him?"

With effort, Margo set her personal distress aside. "Hattie, you hardly know the man. I can't believe I'm hearing this."

"You're young. You can afford to wait around. I can't!"

The pleased look on Hattie's face made Margo soften her voice. "I wouldn't be half surprised if he did. How do you feel about him?"

Hattie's eyes lit up like Roman candles. "I can hardly wait to see him again!"

"Why don't you invite him over for supper sometime?"

"What about Daddy? As soon as he finds out Ed works for the Circle G, he'll put his foot down."

Margo frowned. "I wish I could tell you you're wrong, but . . ."

What would Grandpa say when he found out Margo had spent the day with Rebel? Well, she and Hattie were grown women and they shouldn't go on letting Grandpa Fitz act like a tyrant.

Chapter Eight

The telephone rang. "Margo? Rebel." His deep voice reached up through the depths of the phone, causing her pulse to quicken.

"Hi."

"Thought I'd give you a ring. Wanted to hear your voice again. Are you interested in going for a horseback ride today? I know it's last minute, but my crew finished weeding the vineyards earlier than I expected. We could still get in a late picnic lunch. I'll have Sofia pack something. You'd be doing Jake a favor." He chuckled good-naturedly. "He needs a workout. Haven't had much time for him the last few days. You owe me, don't you think, since you talked me into buying him. Well, what do you say?"

Margo didn't hesitate. "I'd like to very much. What time?"

"Say in an hour?"

"An hour?" she said, incredulous. She had just washed her hair, and Hattie wanted her to help in the vegetable garden. *Oh, what the heck, I can do that to-*

morrow. Besides, she hated gardening—all those little weeds clinging so tenaciously to life.

"Is that too soon?" he asked.

"I'll try to get ready by then." She smiled to herself. "Shall we meet at the end of the alfalfa field?"

"Will do. I've been wanting to ride over to the ancient water marks on the hills above La Quinta. Okay?"

"Sounds fine. It's hard to believe the valley was once under water, isn't it? Maybe we'll find some shells. I used to when I was a kid."

After they hung up, she hurried to find Hattie, then remembered her aunt had gone to the market with Grandpa Fitz. Margo scribbled a note saying she might be late for dinner and left it propped up in front of the fruit bowl on the kitchen table. Through the window, she saw Ned, their foreman, drive by in his pickup. He had already cleaned the remains of the fire.

She scurried down the hall to the bathroom, took out a hair dryer, and ran the hot air through moist strands of hair. Rebel's strong face swam before her. His masculine good looks and Southern charisma had somehow inveigled their way into her heart, even with all her doubts.

The electricity from the dryer caused her hair to dance savagely around her ears like a banshee. When it was nearly dry, she switched off the machine, ran a brush through her hair, and braided it quickly. A pair of clean jeans and a blue-and-white gingham, western-style shirt lay on the bed where she'd left them. She slipped into the garments, then stood back to survey herself in the the cheval mirror. No more of Hattie's chocolate cake! She checked and double-checked her appearance, just to make sure nothing she wore looked too faded or stained.

Grabbing up her boots, Margo tugged them on and rubbed the tops with a cloth. Then she hurried outside to saddle Rouge. The weather was gloriously warm, with only a few clouds in the southeast marring an otherwise clear sky. She swung up on the mare's broad back, adjusted her boots in the stirrups, and let the horse move into a gentle loping gait. It took her only a few minutes to reach the edge of the alfalfa fields.

When Rebel saw Margo approaching, silhouetted against the giant date trees reaching like flowering gifts to the heavens, his mouth twitched into a smile. He sat astride his new horse, Jake. The big animal contentedly nibbled flowering alfalfa heads.

"Sorry I'm late," Margo said, breathless. "Just needed to finish a few things."

Rebel eyed her appreciatively. She looked as fresh as a newly opened daisy. "You're right on time." He let his smile linger. "Ready?"

"Yes. Isn't it a beautiful day?"

He wanted to say, "*almost as beautiful as you*," but merely nodded. He drew the reins to the side of the horse's neck and they moved forward, the horses' hooves almost soundless on the fresh loam. They crossed over onto the sandy desert. Rebel dropped the reins on Jake's neck and folded his arms over his chest, letting the horse pick its own way.

"I love to ride out here," Margo said. She breathed in the clear, fresh air. "I'm so glad you called. It's my day off."

"Seemed too nice to work. And Jake here was getting cabin fever. He told me he wanted out of that stall in the worst way. Hasn't gotten used to the new barn yet. Maybe I'll put a goat in there to keep him company."

She chuckled. "That might work. It's surprising how horses, who roam together in their natural state, can grow fond of having other animals as stall-mates. Give Jake time to adjust."

"Never thought of it quite like that." He leaned over to stroke Jake's lissome neck, as the horses moved along lazily.

Margo hadn't intended to tell him about the fire, or the intruder, but it just spilled out. He was shocked.

"What do you make of it?" she asked.

"I don't know. The sheriff didn't have much to say, then?"

"Maybe he's right, and it was only some homeless person."

"Want me to come over tonight and check around outside?"

"No need. Things will surely calm down now."

"I'll keep my eyes open." He patted her hand reassuringly. Margo's breathing altered with his touch and her heart beat faster.

They had ridden for half an hour when a loud peal of thunder nearly caused their horses to bolt. Like creeping shadows, clouds moved in over the mountains behind them.

"Whoa!" Rebel yelled as Jake spun around. He reached out to try to steady Margo's horse, but she quickly had Rouge in control.

"Where did that come from?" she asked in amazement, glancing behind her at thick gray clouds spread out across the valley.

"I'm afraid we're in for it," Rebel muttered.

"I didn't hear any weather report about a spring rainstorm." She looked around. "There's an old homesteader's deserted house not far from here. Let's run for it."

"Good thinking. We'd better take cover before we get singed by a lightning bolt." He pulled his hat down lower over his forehead and clicked to the horse, who was only too willing to break into a full gallop.

By the time they reached the forlorn rock house, fat raindrops pelted them. They tethered the horses at the far end of the long room and took off the saddles and saddle blankets. The horses nickered nervously and shifted positions.

Margo hugged Rouge's neck, smelling the salty perspiration in her damp, warm mane. "Steady, girl. It's only a little rain." Another peal of thunder sent Rouge shying sideways, her eyes flashing terror, and she bumped into Rebel's gelding.

He grabbed the mare's reins and steadied her. "Whoa, girl!"

Margo soothed her in low tones. Rouge swished her tail, tossed her head, and stamped a hoof on the floor's hard-packed earth. Margo ran her palms over the mare's withers, praying there would be no more thunder. Finally the horse calmed and Rebel handed Margo the reins back.

"This place is about ready to blow away in the next windstorm." He glanced up, warily examining the timbers that supported the old tin roof. "I hope they hold. Must be full of termites from the mushy looks of them." He turned away. "Come sit here by the fireplace, Margo." He pointed to several packing crates stacked in a corner. "I'll break up a couple of those for firewood if we find ourselves stuck for a while." He gave her an encouraging grin.

Rebel didn't mind their predicament at all, since he was with Margo. At least they had food and something to drink.

"It'll blow over soon," Margo said.

He looked around. "I'll make this place a little more comfortable." He squatted down and arranged the saddles and blankets on the floor. "We'll pretend we're sitting on chaise longues in the garden sipping mint juleps back home on the plantation."

She chuckled. "Does that mean you brought along mint juleps?"

He thumbed through the saddlebags. "Sorry, all we've got is a thermos of lemonade and coffee, plus the sandwiches."

She gave him a fake look of disappointment, then knelt on a blanket and pushed against the saddle. He poured lemonade into a plastic cup and handed it to her.

"I am thirsty," she said. "Thanks."

Rebel unpacked the sandwiches Sofia had made. "We'll have our picnic right here. At least there won't be any ants or scorpions."

"You hope! Don't look in the corners."

He laughed easily.

"I'm hungry as a coyote." Margo tucked her legs under her and glanced through the open doorway. The door had long ago disappeared. "At least we'll manage to keep relatively dry until it ends."

"If the roof holds, that is."

She, too, gave it a cautious inspection.

Rebel thought her face looked as soft as a meadow flower. He had an urge to remove each thick section of her braid and let her hair hang free on her shoulders. But he sensed she would consider that to be too intimate. He cherished these moments with her. Strange how fate had played into his hands. He sincerely wanted to build on their budding relationship and hoped she did too.

The rain beat a staccato rat-a-tat against the tin roof, each beat keeping her near him a little longer. He handed her the sandwich Sofia had made and refilled her cup. Margo had brought along some of Hattie's chocolate chip cookies and four red apples.

She rubbed one of them on her jeans. "Two of these are for the horses," she said.

When Margo finished the roast beef and cheese sandwich, she got up and went over to the nervous animals. Rebel stood watching her. The horses seemed calmer, but if the thunder started to clap again, he feared they might kick the walls out of the old building.

With a twist of her palm, Margo tossed one of the apples to Rebel underhanded. "Here, this will make Jake's ears stand up."

Rebel caught it with the ease of a practiced baseball player. Rouge reached out to take the apple from Margo's outstretched fingers, as Rebel fed Jake. The big chestnut chomped his to pieces without dropping a speck. Part of Rouge's landed on the floor and rolled a foot away. When Margo reached down to retrieve it, the mare gave her a nudge with her powerful head, sending Margo flying into Rebel's arms.

He laughed, holding her close for a moment. "You've certainly got that mare trained well."

Margo pulled away. "I ought to eat this other half myself—serve her right," she said in mock anger. Taking a tissue out of her jeans pocket, she wiped the fruit. Rouge lifted her head, rolled her eyes, and stuck out her upper lip. Margo handed the remainder of the apple over and gave the mare a pat on the neck.

Rebel sat down and leaned against a saddle, stretched out his long legs, and crossed an ankle over the other. Margo joined him. The rain continued, heavier now. He thought about what she had told him regarding the intruder. Was the fire a coincidence? Not likely.

He took a bite out of a second sandwich. "Now all we need is a television and we could watch the Lakers."

"Or an old movie," Margo said.

He glanced around the room. The rain dripped through the roof in a few places. "If we had the mariachis here we could dance."

"Here we are in a ramshackle room in the middle of a rainstorm and you're thinking of mariachis." She was still standing. "Let's pretend we can hear them. I'll hum. How about dancing the Mexican Hat Dance?" She began to hum, dancing by herself, smiling down at him. He swung himself up and took her in his arms in a courtly manner.

"Shall I throw my hat down?"

She laughed. "Only if you want to get it dirty. This floor doesn't look like it's been swept in a decade—or maybe an entire century."

They danced. He leaned back to look at her face. "I'm glad we're alone."

His lips touched the top of Margo's ear, sending a tormenting chill down her spine.

She stopped humming and replied honestly, "Me too."

They continued to dance.

He whirled her around and sang in a clear voice, *"You belong to my heart, now and forever. And our love had its start . . ."* Then he stopped. "Darn! I forgot the words."

She chuckled. "You're a fine baritone—something else I've learned about you. Don't stop singing."

"Thanks. I'm rusty, though." Rebel sang another song, holding her close. Something deep inside him told him their relationship was meant to be special. Margo possessed qualities he'd dreamed of in a woman—purity, innocence, and honesty. She was spirited and easy to talk to.

All at once, she pulled away, her brows drawing into a frown. "Rebel, I don't think . . ."

He cleared his throat, not wanting to hear what he knew she'd say. "I apologize for getting us stranded. You probably have lots of things to do other than be stuck here with me."

His words broke the tension.

"It's not your fault," she said lightly. "Heaven knows, it doesn't often rain in the desert. Let's look at it as an adventure."

"I like that—an adventure."

Outside, thunder and lightning continued, echoing through his heart and mind as she returned to his arms. They began to dance again to the tunes she sang this time. But like him, she soon forgot the words. Her voice hummed in his ear, her sweet breath caressing his cheek.

They sat down and leaned against the saddles once more. Unable to resist the impulse, he reached over and took her hand. Surely that was safe enough, he thought. Turning up her palm, he kissed the pink flesh. Her hand was small and delicately shaped, her fingers beautifully tapered. A single turquoise silver ring encircled one finger.

"This is the hand that performs miracles on injured animals," he said.

She didn't speak but smiled, watching him.

Swallowing hard, he let go of her hand and heaved himself up. The room had dimmed. "I'll light a fire now." He plucked a box of matches off a dusty shelf and dropped them in his pocket. Then he set about dismantling the wooden crates. It took several attempts before a weak fire took hold.

"At least the horses have settled," Margo said.

He dropped down beside her and laid his head against the saddle, looking at her. "I could get used to this. No worries. No responsibility You beside me."

"It would be grand." Her eyes softened, and he was surprised when she said, "I don't hold your wanting our land against you, Rebel, even though Grandpa does."

He shot up to a sitting position. "Maybe he'll come around to realizing I'm not really a land-grabber. Making an offer didn't seem like such a horrible thing to do when I sent the letter. It's done all the time." He let his mouth turn up in an amused grin.

They settled back down again. Time ticked away, their conversation lengthening, as night slipped by unnoticed. She moved closer into the crook of his arm. They talked about their childhood, favorite movies, and the music they liked best.

"I see we have things in common other than horses and farming," he said, his lips brushing her forehead. She felt so good he couldn't resist. "My own granddad dominated my boyhood, somewhat like yours. But I'll have to admit that it was a pretty good life."

"Grandpa can be awfully overbearing," she admitted, "but I love him dearly all the same."

Rebel held her a moment longer, then backed off. "Maybe we should have a cup of coffee." Margo's voice was a bare whisper.

He smiled. "Yeah, I'll get the thermos. Tired?"

"Very. I must look bleary-eyed," Margo said. She attempted to push back a strand of hair that fell over one eye.

"You look beautiful."

She grinned.

Rebel reached over and helped her to her feet. He couldn't resist pulling her into his arms, his lips pressing warmly on her temple. His fingers held the back of her head with possessive authority for a brief moment as he kissed her, then he released his hold. "The rain has stopped," he said, smiling down into her eyes.

Margo was the first to break eye contact. She crossed the floor to the doorway and looked out. The softness of mist scented air. "Yes, it finally stopped raining." She glanced around and sighed, while trying to recapture the cradle of enchantment the little one-room house had created. "I'll remember this place forever."

Rebel stood behind her and wrapped his arms around her waist. She turned to face him. His eyes were luminous, his dark hair slightly tousled. A wreath of cool, clean air blew through the open door, encircling them.

"You could come back to my ranch, Margo. Sofia would cook us a big dinner—ham and fixin's."

Margo's stomach rumbled. "Stop it. You're making me even hungrier. Right now I'm willing to try most anything—even a calorie-laden dinner like that."

"Then you'll come back to my place?"

"You know I can't do that. If my grandfather finds

out I'm here with you, I'm done for. He'll probably force us into a shotgun wedding." She chuckled.

He leaned his head back and laughed delightedly. "Would that be so terrible?"

His remark caught her off guard. She was just trying to be funny. "Uh, we hardly know each other," she stammered.

He started to say something but she cut him off. "We'd better get a move on." Turning her back to him, she hurried over to Rouge and began to saddle the mare.

By the time he had finished saddling Jake, the valley was awash in sparkling sunlight. Margo glanced back over her shoulder at the old rock house. In the light of day it looked so forsaken. They had shared something memorable inside those four walls—earth-shaking kisses and confidences that had lulled her into a serene glow. All at once, her future seemed to loom like a bright, dazzling meteor, her heart reaching out on a golden beam to him as he rode alongside her. The velvety hush of the storm's departure now promised lovely weather.

Can this be how falling in love feels?

The horses were eager to run, ready to feel the cool breeze in their manes. But Margo and Rebel sank back in the saddles, slowing them down, not willing to shorten the time on their way home. He turned and leaned sideways in the saddle. Reaching out, his hand closed around hers. The last hours seemed unreal—like a wonderful dream she didn't want to end. He kissed her quickly, his eyes glittering.

"If you keep kissing me like that we'll never get home," she chastised him with a feigned frown.

His mouth turned up in a mischievous grin. "I promise not to kiss you again if you swear you'll let me take you to dinner tomorrow night and the next night and the next?"

Margo chuckled. "Be serious. Besides, I'm not sure I'm ready for romance. It's so—I don't know, emotionally challenging."

He eyed her keenly. "You know that's only partly true."

She burst into laughter. "All right. I'll have dinner with you tomorrow."

"At seven. Chinese? Pasta? Mexican food?"

"Surprise me. I love surprises." *And you're the biggest surprise of all*, she thought with happiness.

They rode on. Margo had never seen the hues of the sky quite so brilliantly blue after a rain. It reminded her of Rebel's eyes. She turned to give his sculpted profile a sidelong glance. He was a contrast of strength and tenderness, seriousness and humor—endearing qualities in any man.

Rebel threw her a grin and pushed back his hat. The wondrous afternoon with Margo had left him adoring her more than ever. However, he did feel their relationship had changed from friendship to something far more meaningful.

The sun spun gold lights in her hair as her horse loped slightly ahead of him.

When Margo got up the next morning, Hattie had just finished mixing pancake batter in a big metal bowl in the kitchen.

"Go for an early-morning ride, did you?" Hattie eyed her niece speculatively.

"Yes. And I'm starving. Let me help you fix breakfast."

"Sure. Get out the griddle."

Margo's mouth watered. She pulled off her boots and stood them up in the corner, padding across the kitchen in her stocking feet.

"I went to a movie with Ed last night," Hattie said, amazing Margo. "Such a gentleman! Said I'm as pretty as a desert flower."

"Oh, I'm glad you had a good time." Margo smiled, lifting the griddle off one of the lower cupboard shelves.

"I know I'm past fifty but he makes me feel like I'm twenty again." Hattie giggled, throwing Margo an affectionate grin.

Hattie's exuberance added to Margo's own euphoria, even if it left her a little bewildered. Her aunt had been stuck in the past for so long, and now she seemed to be metamorphosing before Margo's very eyes.

Hattie became serious. "I'm going to do what I want for a change! What a waste my life has been! Don't you make the same mistake, missy."

Margo was on the verge of sharing with her aunt the circumstances of the day before when Hattie said, "Ed told me something interesting about his boss."

"Oh?"

"Rebel's fiancée is arriving this weekend." Her voice sounded casual, but her eyes watched Margo.

Stunned, Margo almost dropped the griddle. Rebel Gentry engaged! Knowing her aunt was expecting a reply, she expelled an unsteady breath, her eyes burning. "I'm glad you had a good time."

"You look sort of pale. Now, you aren't coming down

with something? Ought to take better care of yourself. You work too hard, what with all those emergencies."

Margo barely heard Hattie's last words, and she set the griddle down with a thud on the countertop. With trembling fingers, she turned away to pour herself a cup of coffee, fighting to mask the hurt clawing at her. She cared for a man who was not available. But after yesterday, how was she to rein in her heart? Anger followed on a wave of agony. If he was engaged, then why didn't he tell her, and why did he kiss her with such emotion? He must be as unscrupulous as Kane—a scoundrel who wanted to use her! How could a woman trust *any* man?

"Margo?"

She bit her lip so hard it hurt. "I don't think I'm hungry after all. Maybe I've got a touch of the flu coming on." She blew her aunt a kiss and started out of the room.

Hattie smiled warmly. "You haven't done that since you were a teenager."

"Shame on me, then. I do love you dearly, Hattie." She fought back tears.

Hattie came over to give Margo a hug. "Bless you, child, you might as well have been my own daughter. You surely know that. And don't I say a prayer every day for you? Go along now. We'll talk later when you're feeling more chipper."

"Yeah," Margo almost whispered. But she knew she wouldn't. Sometimes she could open her heart to those she loved, but for some reason, it didn't come naturally to her. Animals were easy to love. They were utterly accepting and couldn't ask questions. But people were different. They had long memories.

She sat the coffee cup on the counter and rushed down the hall to her bedroom, locked the door, and sprawled on the bed, drawing up her knees. Feeling utterly betrayed, she let the misery sweep over her.

Chapter Nine

During the night hours, Margo thrashed the sheets until they were wadded around her hips. Bitter thoughts tramped through her mind in an endless succession. Wetting her lips, she told herself, *I guess I'm a slow learner, otherwise, how could I be so gullible?*

Her attraction to Rebel must have muddled her thinking. She had taken him for a strong, decent, and honorable man. But if he were all those things, wouldn't he have said he was committed to another woman? It was hard for her to believe someone she cared about could be without scruples.

Frustrated with trying to sleep, Margo rolled off the mattress and plunked her feet firmly on the floor. She glanced down at the bed. It looked as though a tornado had whipped its treacherous winds around her during the night and gobbled her up.

For years she had shied away from romantic entanglements. Fearful of surrendering her personal identity, of being controlled by another, and fearful of rejection, she'd made her own way alone. Now, having learned that Rebel had a fiancée, it only reinforced her deep-seated anxieties.

Margo glanced out the bedroom window, for once not hearing the birds sing or taking in a breath of the blossom-filled, early morning air. She turned away. Not wanting to see her family, she dressed hurriedly and drove straight to the clinic, hoping to get lost in her work.

Grace came in at 8:00 and poked her head in Margo's office. Margo had already updated a stack of files. Grace looked slightly bedraggled but cheerful nonetheless. She looked at Margo and frowned. "Morning, Doc. I'll put the coffee on. You look like you could use a cup."

Margo thanked her.

In a little while Grace brought a mug of coffee, along with several messages, and placed them on the metal desktop.

Margo took a sip of the brew, ignoring the slips of paper with the messages. "You're right. This is just what I needed."

Grace smiled and went back to the reception desk. Margo slipped on a white coat. She sat down at the desk again, exhausted—and the work day had only begun. Absently chewing a pencil eraser, she bent over the messages, trying to decide which one to call back first. Then she realized she'd read the same message at least three times. Her head felt groggy from lack of sleep. Nothing meant anything. She felt sad, angry, hurt—all rolled into one.

An hour later, Grace rushed into her office in a stew, a note pad clutched in her hand.

"Emergency, Doc! A cattle truck overturned on the freeway near the Salton Sea. The sheriff's dispatcher said steers fell out and are wandering off. There's complete mayhem over there. The sheriff's asking for all able-bodied horsemen in the area to volunteer to help track the cattle. A relief truck's on its way. They need a vet, too. Can you go? I've got the dispatcher on hold."

"Tell them I'm on my way."

Margo's first concern was for the injured animals, but she knew the occasion promised to be an old-fashioned roundup, and that excited her. She hadn't participated in anything like it since a herd of cattle got lost in the San Jancinto Mountains when she had been a teenager.

"And don't forget to tell Dr. Thornsey where I'm going," she called as Grace hurried out.

Margo grabbed medical supplies and equipment, and rushed home to get her horse.

Rouge needed little coaxing to get into the horse trailer. Margo slid behind the steering wheel, fastened the seat belt, and headed down the long drive.

When she arrived at the accident scene, she flashed on her turn signal. Lying on its side, the truck looked like a giant toy a child had carelessly discarded. A makeshift holding pen had been set up for the cattle. Horsemen were adjusting saddle cinches and forming into small groups. She backed Rouge out of the trailer, slung the medical bag over the back of the saddle, and tied it securely. The picture before her was one of chaos. Several steers lay dead beside the road. With a heavy heart, she mounted and turned her horse in the direction of the riders.

Sheriff Stoney squinted at Margo and raised his gloved hand. He had a rifle and a rope attached to the front of his saddle.

"Looks like some of the steers smelled water and are

heading toward the Salton Sea," he boomed over the voices of the riders and the traffic passing by. "We want to prevent that if we can. The saltwater'll kill 'em if they don't get hit by a car first." He looked around. "Everybody ready? Okay, let's take off. Need to travel fast. Watch for tracks. And for heaven's sake be careful of the prairie-dog holes. Don't want any broken legs."

He swung his hat in the air with authority. The sun bounced off his official badge. Then he turned back in the saddle as his horse trotted off in the direction of the large body of water. Although it was actually a lake, it had been named a sea because of its salt content.

Margo noticed some of the men were Native Americans from the nearby Torres-Martinez Indian Reservation, and she was acquainted with two of them. They exchanged nods.

Just then someone rode up alongside her. " 'Morning, Margo!"

Without turning her head, she recognized Rebel's deep baritone voice, and her heart did a double beat. She gave him a vague smile and muttered a noncommittal "Hi."

"I thought I might find you out here," he said. "Never a dull moment for a vet, I suppose."

Margo felt her face turn to granite. If she never smiled again, it would be his fault. How dare he act so casual!

Rouge reached over to nip Rebel's horse on the neck. Jake jumped sideways, almost unseating him.

"Whoa!" he ordered.

Margo brought Rouge up and looked him square in the face. "I guess my horse doesn't like yours very much," she said, her tone purposely spiteful.

His eyes widened. "Margo, I . . ."

"We really don't have time to talk." Without another word, she let Rouge break into a gallop, catching up to the group of horsemen ahead, leaving Rebel trailing behind. She could taste her irritation like alum on the tongue.

Rebel shook his head, wondering what had caused her to turn into an ice princess. Her unexpected rebuff roiled him clear down to his booted heels. He took off his cowboy hat and raked his fingers through the strands of his hair, then clamped the hat back on his head and clicked to his horse.

He caught up to Margo but she didn't give him so much as a glance. She rode well, her body moving in sync with the horse's movements. Watching her caused his blood to stir when he recalled the sweet taste of her lips. He had fallen hard for the lady, but for some unknown reason she was giving him the cold shoulder this morning. And she had canceled their dinner date, leaving a hasty message on the answering machine.

The sheriff continued to lead the riders. Over the rumble of horses' hooves beating the sandy earth, Rebel called out to him. "Why don't I take a couple of these men and head south. Chances are the cattle have spread toward one of the farms or over toward the reservation."

Sheriff Stoney had pulled his horse up. "Good thinking," he replied. He leaned back in the saddle and called to two men on his left. "Follow this man."

Rebel wasn't finished. "How about having the vet come along with us?"

"Okay." The sheriff motioned to Margo. "You go with them, Dr. Fitzgerald."

Her first impulse was to yell hotly, *"I will not!"* However, Jeb Tyson, a rancher she disliked, stood up in his stirrups, watching her, a smirk on his weather-beaten face. She knew it would arouse speculation if she didn't follow the sheriff's directions.

"Well, I hope these steers have been inoculated against anthrax," she said with a straight face.

The sheriff groaned but didn't answer. Jeb dropped back in the saddle, his smirk turning to fear, and hurried to catch up with another group. Margo moved Rouge out and smiled to herself. The possibility of anthrax had to be pretty remote.

They took off at a quick pace. Plenty of hard work lay ahead. Whenever thoughts of being marooned with Rebel in the little rock house tried to take over, Margo forced them down. He rode just ahead, tall in the saddle. She kept Rouge back on purpose. *Let Rebel play the big leader.* However, she soon forgot personal considerations in the excitement of the chase. They had to divert the cattle away from the saltwater. But her main concern was the injured steers she might encounter along the way.

The small group passed through several arroyos before Margo found a dead steer lying on its side. She shook her head, hoping the others were still alive.

"Let's move on," Rebel said. "Nothing we can do here." His body swayed in a rocking motion as his horse sprang forward.

The hard riding made Rouge washy with sweat and she grunted. Surely they would be catching up to some of the live steers soon, Margo thought. Blowing wind from the east kicked up dust. She took out a handkerchief and tied it bandit-style over the lower part of her face for protection.

Just beyond a rise, with the Salton Sea not more than

a quarter of a mile away, Rebel spotted a solitary herd of frightened steers spread out near a sand dune. "Over here," he called.

The riders worked to herd them together. Rebel slapped his coiled rope against his leg, shouting guttural urgings to the bawling strays.

Knowing he wasn't a cattleman, Margo couldn't help but be impressed with the way he handled them. She moved Rouge to and fro behind the cattle, as woman and horse worked in unison to prevent stragglers from escaping.

Rebel twisted in the saddle, eyeing her sharply. Suddenly he dashed off to catch a recalcitrant steer that had done an about-face. In less than a minute the steer trotted dutifully back to the others. Margo shook her head, smiling in spite of herself. "Not bad riding for a tenderfoot," she said.

Rebel grinned. He turned to the other men and slipped off one of his gloves. "You take these back and we'll push on. The relief truck should be here by now."

They nodded in agreement and coaxed the steers into moving forward together.

"Let's go, Margo," Rebel said. He didn't wait for her reply but whirled Jake around. Margo followed without a word. They continued to search over dunes and down every wash in the vicinity.

Without warning, Margo propelled out of the saddle when Rouge went down on both knees. Like a bale of hay, Margo found herself tossed up on the side of a wavy sand dune, glad she wasn't staring down a sidewinder. Stunned, she sat there a moment, knowing she must look like a frightened blue-jeans mess, her hair hanging partly loose from its braid. She slipped off the handkerchief, which haphazardly covered one eye. And when she tried to rise, she let out a cry, clutching her shoulder. A few feet away, the mare gamely got back up, snorting.

Rebel's face registered complete horror as he jumped from his horse and raced to Margo's side. "You okay?" He bent over her, his mouth set in a grim line, his hands reaching out to her.

Margo tried to get up again and failed. She moaned as a stab of pain ricocheted through her shoulder.

Rebel dropped down on a knee. "Just a minute! Let's make sure nothing's broken first." He carefully helped her to a sitting position, his eyes searching her face.

Margo spat out sand. "I'm okay." She cautiously rolled her injured shoulder. "Rouge must have stepped in a darn hole. Glad it wasn't a snake's."

"Yeah. Rouge's fine, but I'm not so sure about you." His eyes filled with concern. "I'll get my canteen. You'll want to wash the sand out of your mouth."

"Thanks." Hating the grit in her teeth, she spat again. The shock of the fall caused her muscles to turn to jelly.

Rebel came back and poured water into his canteen cup, handing it to her. He slipped a handkerchief out of his back pocket and brushed dirt away from her forehead. Margo washed her mouth out.

"Better?"

She met his level gaze. "I think so." Her breath came easier, but pain shot down her arm.

"You're hurt," he insisted. "Do you think you dislocated your shoulder? We could call for an ambulance."

"That won't be necessary. I think it's just bruised. Only my pride's injured." Handing back the cup, she attempted to stand.

"Oh, sure. You're lucky you didn't break your neck!" he fussed, insisting on helping her.

His arms wrapped around her like a gentle bear's, and he swept her up with the comforting strength of one who works with his hands. Reluctant to let her go, he held her a moment, scrutinizing her face. Then he leaned down impulsively and kissed the top of her head before setting her on her feet.

"Thank goodness you're still sound, Margo," he murmured, brushing dust from her hair. "I couldn't stand the thought of you getting hurt bad."

Margo, speechless, saw him swallow hard with emotion, and found herself doing the same. He handed her a slightly crumpled hat and dirty sunglasses. "I ought to take you home and buy you a new straw hat," he said.

"I have no intention of going home, thank you," she said, having recovered most of her dignity. She took the hat and the sunglasses and clapped them on. "Stop hovering over me. I'll be fine." Then realizing she was being rude, she tried to smile. "Thanks for the help."

She limped over to Rouge and checked the mare briefly for injuries. Satisfied, Margo emptied the sand out of her moccasins and mounted painfully before he could lend a hand. He stood there, his mouth set.

"Shouldn't we be going?" she said.

"Now, Margo, you really ought to go home. You're hurt."

She felt ashamed at how she had treated him. "If I had to take a tumble, I'm glad I fell into a sand dune—and you were here."

Rebel didn't grin. "You ought to win a bronze spur after all this."

"A bronze spur?" She chuckled. "Sounds like you're

talking about an Olympic medal." His touching words made her want to forgive him for the other night, but it didn't last long. He had a lot of explaining to do. Engaged! But this was neither the time nor the place to bring up the subject.

"Let's go now," she said, and turned her horse away without waiting for him.

By dusk, the cattle had been rounded up and loaded aboard the waiting truck. Sheriff Stoney invited everyone to meet him at the roadhouse to celebrate, the same place where Kane had taken Margo. Instead of joining the party, she drove straight home.

Rebel searched for Margo amid the men standing around in the roadhouse, two cold bottles of Coke in his hands. Dusty jeans and perspiration-stained cowboy hats attested to their day in the saddle. Large bowls of pretzels were set on the tables to ward off hunger until the chili could be brought from the kitchen. Rebel set the bottles down, took a handful of pretzels and popped one in his mouth. The salt increased his thirst and he took a sip of Coke out of one of the bottles.

He had stayed behind until the last steer was safely stowed on the truck. It took him a little time to realize Margo wasn't among the others. Funny, he had thought she would relish this sort of gathering, since she knew most of the valley ranchers. Then an uneasy feeling stirred in his gut. Something was definitely wrong between them. But he tried to tell himself it wasn't true. Perhaps seeing the dead steers depressed her, he thought, rubbing the back of his neck with both hands. There wasn't a lot even the healing hands of an experienced vet could do. Baffled, he picked up the bottle again and downed the Coke, almost chugalugging. He couldn't picture her as the kind of woman who blew hot and cold, yet why had she acted so contentiously? The frightening notion that she might have been hurt in the fall more than she let on made his stomach to turn over.

"Shoot!" he muttered, jerking open the door to go outside. He didn't want to stay if she wasn't here.

Rebel headed for the Range Rover and jumped in, dirty and stiff and sore from riding all day. He slammed the door, turned on the engine, and rolled down the window. Jake whinnied in the trailer behind. "Okay, boy," he called back. "We're heading for the barn."

Chapter Ten

The following morning Margo was back to work at the clinic, her shoulder still aching. Grace handed her a slip of paper when she came out of surgery to retrieve something she needed.

She glanced at it and frowned. "Grace, if Mr. Gentry calls back, tell him I'm busy."

When the receptionist left her alone, Margo jammed the note in the pocket of her green surgical uniform. He had called three times the night before. She opened a cabinet, and with an unsteady hand, took a vial off the shelf. Ever since hearing Rebel was engaged, she hadn't been herself.

Margo joined Dr. Thornsey in the operating room. An anesthetized quarter horse was waiting, hoisted in a giant sling.

"We probably won't need the extra medication but we ought to have it here just in case," he said.

Margo placed the vial on a countertop, slipped on surgical gloves, and set about assisting him. With the utmost care they proceeded to sever a nerve in the animal's hoof, which had been causing it to go lame. The practice of equine medicine had come a long way, Margo thought as she worked. Ten years ago this operation would have been touch-and-go. Now they would be able to restore the animal to reasonably good health.

When the operation was completed, Dr. Thornsey smiled. He tore off his gloves and ran his palms together. "We've done it! This fella's going to be as good as new."

His enthusiasm always amused Margo. He took a personal delight in making animals well, and she understood where he was coming from. Animals brought great joy.

She thought about the book, *All Creatures Great and Small*. It could have been written by Dr. Thornsey.

Margo returned to her office, slipped out of the surgical uniform, and donned a white coat. Before dumping the uniform in a hamper, she thrust her fingers into the pocket for Rebel's message.

It was basically the same as the others he'd sent.

Margo,
Please call as soon as possible. We need to talk.
                                                    Rebel

Well, she wasn't going to call—ever! She didn't owe him any explanations. It was the other way around. Let him enjoy his fiancée's visit! *Who knows, maybe they'll elope to Las Vegas!* She didn't care a fig! Her life already overflowed without him, and she made a hurried vow to keep it that way. But after a while an uneasiness pricked at her heart, and she knew she was a liar.

Grace stuck her blond head in Margo's office before closing time. "Phone's for you, Doc," she said.

Preoccupied, Margo glanced up. Grace surveyed her with a curious glint in her eyes. Margo knew she'd sound odd demanding to know if it was Rebel on the phone again. After all, she didn't make a practice of having the receptionist screen her calls.

Grace shifted her stance, waiting. Although the attractive young woman hadn't reached her twenty-first birthday, she wore a lovely engagement ring. Margo, on the other hand, didn't even have a steady beau. The thought sent her mood plummeting. Her professional life might be on the ascent but her personal life was mired right down there in the doldrums.

"Doc, should I take another message or not?"

Margo cleared her throat. "Thanks, no. I'll take it." She stretched her arm over the desk to retrieve the phone. "Hello, Dr. Fitzgerald speaking."

A vaguely familiar male voice said, "Margo, this is Michael Jonson. I've called you a couple of times but we never seem to connect." His tone was as smooth as molasses. "I'd like to get together with you soon. How about dinner tomorrow night? I have an important proposition."

"Can't you tell me what it is over the phone?" She waited, cradling the receiver slightly away from her ear, and swiveled the chair from side to side.

"Uh, it would be so much better if we could mix business with a little enjoyment. I know a great French restaurant in Palm Springs."

Michael oozed charm, vaguely arousing her curiosity. What could he be offering this time?

"I'm terribly busy right now," she said coolly. "Perhaps if you fax me the information I can discuss it with my grandfather. This *is* regarding the ranch, isn't it?" Before he could reply, she said, "Good-bye, Mr. Jonson." His fast-talking remarks and little deceits disgusted her, and she would as soon have dinner with him as with a billygoat.

After Margo hung up, she grasped the edge of the desk so hard she was in danger of breaking her fingernails. He and his cohorts! She wished she'd never met any of them.

Many years ago her grandfather had deeded half of the ranch to her father. Then she had inherited his half. But she and Grandpa Fitz were in complete agreement with regard to it. She glanced around her office. Coming back home last year had proven to be a good idea—and she loved her work. Why couldn't it be enough?

Margo prayed their farm agent, Ben Carlton, would soon find a buyer for the alfalfa crop. With hard work and a little luck, she'd pull the ranch through for another year. Farming could be a ticklish occupation, but owning one's own land had its rewards.

Taking up the chart she'd set aside, she hurriedly entered pertinent information, then filed it away. It was time to go home.

Margo hurried out to the Cherokee, slammed it in gear, and tore out of the parking lot. She enjoyed the convenience of the sport utility vehicle enormously, and didn't want to think she might have to sell it to help pay off the taxes. Oh well, there was always Grandpa's old truck to get around in. The thought depressed her.

When Margo arrived home, she went directly to her bedroom and grabbed riding boots off the floor in the closet, mindful of dried mud she hadn't cleaned on the heels. She needed to get off by herself. Fortunately, her shoulder felt miraculously better. In less than a minute, she'd slipped off her denim dress and pulled well-worn jeans on. Carrying the boots, she trooped down the hall to the kitchen.

Hattie hummed an old western tune. *"The sage in bloom, is like perfume, deep in the heart of Texas."* She glanced up from where she sat at the table peeling potatoes, and cast a maternal smile at her niece.

"Hi, sweety," she said. "Feeling better? You've had a time of it. First the flu, then your shoulder."

Margo sighed. "I'm okay, but I've had better days. Hope yours was good."

Her aunt grinned. "Not bad, except for Daddy fussing. He wants to plant a fig tree outback where the shed burned. I want to plant more roses."

"I'm going riding for a while, Hattie. Need some fresh air. See you in an hour or so."

Margo hurried to the stables, saddled Rouge, and mounted. She pressed her knees against the mare's ribs and they ambled off down the dirt road leading in the direction of the grapefruit grove, away from the alfalfa fields. Rouge pricked her ears forward. Margo hunched in the saddle, letting the mare have her head.

She glanced up to the foothills where ancient Indian fish traps nestled into the boulders. They were created in ancient times to catch fish when the Coachella Valley, now a desert, had been under water. And she wondered if that long-ago era was as complex as life today.

Margo stood up in the stirrups and turned to gaze back at the changing countryside. Rouge whinnied, followed by an answering whinny not far away. A rider materialized from the tall shadows of the grapefruit grove. Margo held her breath, frightened it might be the intruder. Transfixed, she shielded her eyes from the sun and strained to see.

Astride his new gelding, Rebel rode lazily toward her. He nonchalantly peeled a grapefruit, tossing the rinds on the furrowed ground.

"You!" she said.

"Hello there." He finished the grapefruit and wiped his big hands on the thighs of his jeans. A stubble of beard covered his jaws. "The only trouble with snitching your fruit is ending up with sticky fingers. You don't have a napkin, do you, Doc?"

"Afraid not," she said in a cutting voice.

He lounged in the saddle, her knight in shining armor. No, he was Mr. Wrong from the get-go. It still bothered her that they had been so romantic at the rock house. She had thought he really cared for her, then. Men could be so fickle. Well, she'd never allow him to play with her feelings again!

"I've been trying to reach you, Margo," he said.

Her stomach muscles knotted and she almost sputtered in righteous rage, *How could you kiss me when you're supposed to be engaged!*

She guessed a gal had to kiss a lot of frogs before she found a real prince. Seeing him hunched over the pommel like a relaxed panther, his dark blue eyes hooded, only confused her. She kept a tight rein on the impatient Rouge. The breeze whipped her hair in her eyes and she reached up, impatiently pushing it back.

Rebel smiled broadly. "You look absolutely beautiful today, Margo," he said, his eyes searching hers.

Commanding her heart to stop thumping so wildly,

she said with a catch in her throat, "Thanks. I see you're riding Jake. Is he working out all right?"

"He's great. Mind if I ride along? Looks like your horse isn't going to stand still much longer."

"I'm going over to check on the alfalfa fields," she lied. "And I'm terribly busy. Another time, maybe."

His smile faded and he looked hurt. "Since you couldn't go to dinner with me, how about later tonight? I left a message at the clinic but apparently you didn't receive it." His hands resting on the saddle pommel.

"Gosh, I can't, Rebel." Knowing full well his fiancée was coming, she added as an afterthought, "How about Saturday? I'm free, then."

He coughed, hesitating a moment. "Wish I could, but company's coming."

Before she could stop herself, Margo stabbed at him with a finger and blurted, "Yes! Your fiancée's coming! I heard all about it. What a ladies' man you are, Rebel Gentry!"

Her words hung in the air like a stinging wasp, and his brows flew together in a dark frown. At first he didn't speak, then said in a low voice, "News travels fast in the valley."

Margo whirled on him, her heart racing. "I think you're despicable! Why didn't you tell me you were engaged? And you kissed me! I thought you cared, when all along you were engaged to another woman. Well, you certainly made a fool out of me without hardly trying."

Rebel winced at her angry remarks, and his intense stare seared her. "Listen to me, Margo! You don't know what you're talking about."

"You listen," she snapped, holding herself together by

sheer force of will. "I trusted you!" She gulped, tasting bile. "My aunt told me all about your fiancée coming!"

He flinched. "Hold on! She's my *ex*-fiancée. I broke up with Roxanne before I left New York. Out of the blue she left a message with Sophia saying she intended to come this weekend. When I tried to call her back, she was out. And like you, she didn't return my call. Since our parting was amiable I assumed she wants a little vacation out here in California. Don't ask me why—I don't know."

"You expect me to believe this, Rebel?"

He nodded. "It's the truth."

Margo's emotions were only partly mollified. She had also put herself in an odd position, since they didn't have an understanding. Now she was embarrassed. "I can't talk to you anymore."

She spun Rouge around and galloped off, leaving Rebel in the dust. But his haunted look of consternation followed her. Before she got back to the house, the sky grayed and wind-gusts kicked up a fine film of sand, a mirror image of her emotions. She reached up to wipe away the tears with her gloved hand. They left splotches on the beige leather, as dark as her heart.

Rebel sat stone rigid in the saddle, watching Margo recede into the distance. Her sharp-edged words threw him for a loop. Weary, he dropped his head into his hands, slowly letting out his breath. When he straightened, he cursed fate. The gelding shifted, straining to go. Rebel pulled the reins to the left, nudged the horse, and took off at a fast clip in the opposite direction from Margo.

Women! Yet in her anger, he'd seen a raw-edged vulnerability. She had to care deeply or she wouldn't have been so incensed. He knew, too, that still waters run deep.

For the rest of the day Rebel immersed himself in ranch duties, trying not to feel anything. Yet Margo's beautiful face swam before him, her cinnamon-tinted eyes, her sweet mouth, the way she laughed. How was he going to get her to believe him?

When Margo reached home, she retreated to the study, feeling even worse than when she'd left. She sank into the captain's chair at the roll-top desk and tapped her lower lip with her index finger, trying to think with some sort of logic. A stack of her grandfather's old Zane Grey western books rested beside the desk at her feet, and she accidentally kicked them over.

Leaning down to straighten them, she looked up to see Hattie come in.

"Thought you were back," her aunt said. "You must be hungry, hon. Got a tunafish sandwich here and a mug of herb tea." She sat the platter on the desk in front of her. "Go on. Eat."

"I am sort of hungry. Thanks, Hattie." Margo reached for the mug. "You're so good to me. Sometimes I feel downright guilty."

"No need," her aunt said, smiling. But she didn't move to leave. "Want to talk?"

Margo shook her head and stared at a faded photograph of the ranch's original date tree hanging on the wall. "That tree looked so small," she said.

"Well, it's a giant now."

Margo picked up the framed picture of her grandmother Mary on the desk. "Grandma always dressed in a starched apron and she'd bring me a freshly baked cookie right out of the oven. You look very much like her, Hattie. I miss her a lot."

"We all do. Now eat your sandwich."

Margo grinned and picked it up. Hattie made an excuse to leave when she realized Margo wasn't in the mood to talk.

A part of Margo wished her aunt would stay. She was a level-headed and forthright woman. However, Margo couldn't bring herself to confide her problems with Rebel to anyone. It hurt too much.

Tons of work lay right there at her fingertips. Why didn't she get to it? She turned on the desk lamp and took a letter from under the stack. Dr. Marshall had confirmed Grandpa Fitz's medical diagnosis. Alzheimer's disease! The very word sent shivers through her. Yet she had been aware that his mental faculties were sliding for a long time. Hattie was the one who didn't want to believe it. Sadly, the symptoms were all too apparent. They would have to deal with the issue soon.

With a heavy sigh, Margo hid the letter, determined to protect him from seeing its glaring contents. She worked past midnight until, bleary-eyed, she rolled down the top of the desk. Her shoulder cramped with little darts of pain that shot up the nerve endings.

"Nothing's certain but death and taxes, my girl," Grandpa Fitz used to say. She remembered how in the old days he'd tell her stories about when he was a boy in Ireland. His own father had been caught up in the Rising and the Troubles in Ireland. Grandpa said his Uncle Patrick knew Michael Collins, the man who fought to make Ireland a free state.

Well, the Fitzpatricks weren't afraid of a good fight.

She heaved herself out of the desk chair and looked around. Too exhausted to walk down the hall to her bedroom, she slumped onto the worn suede couch, slipped an arm behind her head, and stared up at a spider web on a beam in the ceiling. "There must be an alternative to all this, but what?" she whispered morosely into the night.

Hours later Margo awoke with a start, her neck stiff, and went to the kitchen for a glass of milk. She smelled like horsehair and sweat. The big hands on the clock over the refrigerator pointed to half past 2:00. A full moon lingered like a vast searchlight in the night, casting elongated shadows across the table.

Margo didn't bother to switch on the kitchen light. Something drew her to the window. As she peered out, she glimpsed a shadowy figure move into the stables. *Not again!* Who was it this time? Horse rustlers? That sounded like something straight out of a Zane Grey novel, but she didn't find it amusing.

Fear quickly gave way to rage. No one was going to steal her horse or set the stables on fire! She ran to the living room, grabbed up the fireplace poker, then tore through the kitchen and yanked open the door.

"Hey!" she shouted gruffly, trying to sound like a man. "Get the Sam Hill out of there before I shoot the pants off your hide!" She held the poker as though it were a gun. It glimmered menacingly in the moonlight.

A light-haired young man in ill-fitting clothes came out, making stealthy movements. He carried something tucked up under his arm. In the faint light his eyes reflected fear like an alley cat's.

"Git!" Margo shouted.

He broke into a sprint toward the date garden and

bolted out of sight, lost among the tall, thin trees whose thick fronds created an inky blackness beneath them.

Margo stood planted with her knees knocking now that he was gone, glad he mistook her for a man. She heard an engine backfire, and a vehicle peel rubber.

Gradually getting control of herself, she almost laughed as the puzzle slowly unraveled. He could have been the same man responsible for the shed burning down, and apparently wasn't hired by Rebel or Bradford or even Michael. No, he had to be a homeless person, and it wasn't likely he would take a chance on coming back. She breathed easier.

Her anger turned to pity. Nevertheless, she was glad he was gone, and she placed the poker over her shoulder like a soldier's rifle.

Unknown to Margo, Rebel and Ed had been keeping a late-night vigil on the Desert Jade for over a week. Although close to falling asleep where he leaned against a date tree, Rebel saw the intruder coming out of the Fitzgerald stables. Just as he readied himself to dash from cover and tackle him, Margo unexpectedly came out of the house. He lay back, reassessing his options. Then he set a rifle bead on the man, watching. If he made so much as a move toward Margo, Rebel would wing him in the leg, and he knew himself to be a crack shot.

Margo was magnificent, challenging the intruder that way. Right now he'd like to kiss her—and beat the guy to a pulp.

In the next instant, the intruder took off, running straight into Rebel's path. With the tree for cover, he let him barely get passed. Then he seized him from behind, clamping his hand over the man's mouth and twisting his arm behind him. Ed came on the double. They tied his hands and hoisted him to his feet.

"Come on, you," Rebel said, collaring him.

The man, too frightened to speak, tried to run for it, but without success. They dragged him along and tossed him in the back of the Range Rover, then headed for the Circle G.

Inside the barn, Rebel and Ed threw him on a pile of hay and lit a kerosene lamp hanging from a beam. It cast ghostlike specters in the corners. The man appeared more alarmed by the armed men standing over him than he would have been if the sheriff caught him. After all, the sheriff would only book him for trespassing, then release him.

"Start talking," Rebel said, his tone menacingly low. "You the culprit who burned the Fitzgeralds' shack the other night?"

"No, man," the intruder said, his eyes blazing with fear. "I was only looking for a place to sleep."

Ed kicked his leg and held his shotgun menacingly. "Liar! No more—tell the truth!"

"Okay! Okay!" he cried. "This has gotten too big for me. All Michael's paying me is a hundred bucks. It ain't worth this hassle."

Then Rebel recognized him. "Your name's Hank." The young man was a construction worker for the Jonsons. He balled his fists. "Michael put you up to this?"

Hank tugged on the rope around his wrists. "I was just supposed to scare them—let one of the horses loose. Nothing serious. Let me go. You can't prove anything, anyway."

"Tell you what," Rebel said, thinking fast on his feet, "I'll let you go on one condition."

Hank looked wary. "Yeah?"

"Beat it out of town. All right?"

"Yeah, sure, anything. Just let me go."

Rebel untied him. "Ed, drive him to the edge of town and dump him." Then he turned to the young man. "I see your face and I'm hauling you down to the sheriff's station. Got it?"

Hank rubbed his wrists. "I'll do what you say. No problem, man."

Rebel drove directly to Michael Jonson's upscale house in an exclusive neighborhood. Early morning sunlight carpeted the sprawling, dew-laden lawn. He rang the buzzer three times before Michael answered the door.

"What the heck—" Michael said, his hair tousled. "You always call on your friends so early?" He stood back to let Rebel enter the foyer.

"Need to speak to you."

"Come into the living room. I'd offer you a drink but I know it isn't your style."

Rebel didn't smile. "I don't want a thing, just some answers."

"To what?" Michael instantly looked alert, wiping the sleep out of his eyes.

"I know all about it," Rebel said.

Micheal shrugged. "You lost me there."

"You hired that kid, Hank, to scare the Fitzgeralds. Stupid thing to do."

He grinned, not denying it. "I thought it was clever."

Rebel hauled back and slammed a punishing fist into

Micheal's nose, hearing a roar in his own ears as he ached to take the man apart. With an effort of will, he restrained himself. Blood trickled, and Michael squealed in pain.

"Harm the Fitzgeralds and from now on you'll answer to me."

Groaning, Michael grabbed a handful of tissues off a table, holding them to his dripping nose. "I only meant to give them a little nudge to sell. The old man's going bonkers, for heaven's sake. Julie told me all about it. They'll have to sell one way or the other. You're taking this far too serious."

Rebel stretched to his full height. "You got that right. Stay completely away from them or . . ." He searched for the right words. ". . . I'll break your leg next time."

"I think you've broken my nose. You're a hard man, Rebel."

"One other thing. Margo isn't ever to know about any of this. She thinks it was some homeless person." He turned to go, his anger spent.

"You must have been a bully when you were a kid," Michael said insolently.

"We all have our character flaws," Rebel replied, and walked out of the house.

After closing the clinic on Friday, Margo drove to the mall in Indio to pick out a shower gift for Grace on her way home. To her consternation, she spotted Rebel through the window of her favorite boutique. He handed a credit card to the saleslady. A big box rested on the countertop.

Not engaged—ha! Rebel must be buying a present for his fiancée! Who else would he be buying a feminine gift for? Turning on her heel, she dashed furiously out of the building and rushed home to lick her wounds.

Margo collapsed on her bed, her heart pounding, partly in anger and partly in disappointment. She had tried to tell herself that what Rebel told her was true—he wasn't engaged. But now she doubted him all over again. This whole thing was driving her slightly crazy. Where was the self-assured, goal-oriented woman she'd always believed herself to be? And why was she letting this man destroy her presence of mind? Didn't she have more than enough to worry about?

Shortly after opening time, Margo entered the bank for her appointment. She had put on a navy blue dress and platform heels for the occasion—something she didn't feel at all comfortable in. A secretary in a short red suit led Margo to an office where Bill Burnbaum, the loan officer, sat at his desk pushing back a cuticle. He indicated she should take a chair while he picked up his thin-rimmed glasses.

"Margo, this takes me back," he said, bending over his desk to shake her hand before sitting down again. "Remember when we went to high school together? It's been a long time." He put his glasses on, his eyes taking her in. "Understand you're a vet now. Great! Just great! What can I help you with?"

Bill Burnbaum had turned fleshy, with folds under his eyes. Margo swallowed hard, then laid it out plain and simple. "I need a loan to pay the taxes."

"Still living on the ranch, huh?" He shook his head. "The bank's in a squeeze right now. Had to foreclose on too many condominium tracts here in the valley. I can't promise you anything right now but I'll take it up with the committee." He glanced at the papers in her hand. "Ah, I see you've filled them out. Give us a week. Maybe we can do lunch—discuss old times."

She handed him the papers, and clutched her purse tightly. "Then there is a possibility?"

He ran his hand doubtfully over his chin and sighed. "I wish I could say yes, but I can't be more helpful at this point."

Margo rose and he extended his hand again. It felt as soft as bread dough, and he wore a gold band on his finger. "Thanks for talking to me, Bill. It was nice seeing you."

He peered at her over his glasses and grinned. "Keep in touch."

"Believe me, I will," she said with a determined lift of her chin.

Why did nothing seem easy? Her chances of getting the loan seemed slimmer by the minute.

Grace came in just as Margo removed a foxtail from a puppy's paw. "The Circle G Ranch called—an emergency," she said, handing Margo a note. "Doc Thornsey's tied up in surgery."

Margo took the note and glanced down. "Is Mr. Gentry on the phone now?"

"No, it's the ranch foreman. Says a horse is sick. He's a nice old guy."

Margo's sense of duty took priority over hurt feelings. "I'll go, Grace. Tell him I'm on the way."

Margo drove past the imposing Gentry mansion with its majestic neoclassical columns on her way to the stables. She spotted Ed beside a pickup, a toothpick in his mouth, conversing with a young Latino. *He's probably Sofia's son,* she thought, as she pulled on the parking brake. Ed removed his hat. The boy sauntered off. Margo noticed he carried an injured dove in his palm. Another born healer, she thought. Maybe he'd be a vet someday.

Ed opened the door for her. Rebel's bloodhound, sleeping beside the stable entrance, raised its head and managed one rumbling bark before losing interest.

"Hi, Ed. I came as soon as Grace told me you called. What's the problem?"

"Glad you could come right over. Rebel's gone. His buckskin is acting mighty poorly. I thought I better get him looked at, what with the weekend coming up. I know the clinic's closed then."

"You can call me any time of day or night."

"Thanks," Ed said. "Come on inside." He hurried into the stables, sticking his weathered hands into his jeans back pockets. Stalls lined both sides of the neatly tended stables. Jake, Rebel's new horse, leaned over the gate and nickered, his keen eyes watchful. She took a couple of seconds to rub his nose.

When they came to the last stall, Ed peered over the gate and his face grew solemn. Margo followed his gaze, and winced. Rebel's old horse, Henry, swayed, his head scarcely bobbing up as though it was too much effort to hold it erect. Margo entered the stall, placing her hand gently on his thin withers. She recognized the trouble immediately.

"Hello, ol' fella," she said. Then with gentle hands, she lifted his head and peered into his rheumy eyes to confirm the diagnosis.

"Looks like a serious neurological problem," she said.

"It happens to old horses sometimes. He won't be able to stand on his feet much longer and we'll have to put him down pretty soon, I'm afraid." It broke her heart to put one of these wonderful beasts to sleep. Yet to let the horse languish in pain would be even worse. She wished she were tougher.

Ed pinched his mouth together before speaking. "I thought as much. Rebel isn't going to take kindly to this news."

"I wish I didn't have to be the bearer of sad tidings but he needs to know right away. We don't want the gelding to suffer. When Henry goes down, he won't have the strength to get up again."

"Knowing Rebel, he'll want to be with him when he steps over the veil to that great pasture in the sky. It's a darn shame. He was old Mr. Gentry's favorite. Got him when he was a colt. And Rebel took to him right off."

"Medicine can do only so much," Margo said. She ran her hands affectionately along the horse's drooping neck.

"I know it ain't your fault, Doc."

Margo patted Ed on the shoulder, then they walked outside. A burgundy Jaguar drove in and parked. Margo knew it was Rebel's, although he usually drove the Range Rover. A woman bent and gave Rebel's cheek a peck. He unfolded his long legs and got out, concern etching his strong, lean face when he saw Margo.

"I got your message on the cell phone, Ed. Left as soon as Roxanne's jet landed. Traffic's awful coming out of Palm Springs this time of day." His eyes slanted to Margo. "Hi."

She opened her mouth to respond when he abruptly

turned around and threw open the car door for his passenger. A striking woman with jet-black hair slid off the leather seat and thrust her shapely nylon-clad legs out of the car. A sleek, classic cashmere suit hugged the curves of her slim body. However, the expensive garment was totally out of place in the warm eighty-degree weather.

So this was Roxanne Humphreys, Rebel's fiancée! When Margo tried to smile she realized her face had frozen, her mouth still open. She chided herself for acting like a teenager in the presence of a movie star. Embarrassed, she cleared her throat.

Roxanne moved elegantly to Rebel's side, a fur coat draped across one arm. Margo tried not to stare but couldn't help herself. Roxanne was a knockout. Rebel took the coat and handed it to Ed. Margo could tell at a glance that it wasn't faux fur, and she bristled. Killing innocent animals to put on one's back raised her hackles. An instant dislike, coupled with the onset of jealously, engulfed her like a prairie fire.

"Roxanne," Rebel said, "this is Dr. Fitzgerald and my foreman, Ed Granger. Roxanne Humphreys."

Margo nodded politely and said hello.

"Howdy, ma'am," Ed said, tipping his hat.

The woman barely acknowledged him, her eyes moving methodically over Margo. "I'm so thrilled to meet you. I understand Rebel's darling horse is sick." Her voice was low, breathy.

"Yes, I'm afraid so." Margo turned to Rebel. She kept her own voice calm, but inside she was shaking with hostility. "Perhaps we could discuss Henry's condition in the stable."

"Right," he replied. "Will you excuse me, Roxanne?

I need to see about my horse. Ed will take you to the house."

Margo saw the concern etched on his face as he turned away from his guest. They had gone only a few steps when Roxanne called, "Rebel, darling, you've penciled in a party while I'm here, haven't you? I want to meet all your friends." With her gaze fixed on Margo, she said grandly, "You simply must come too, Doctor. I've never met a lady veterinarian. How quaint! You can tell me how you came to take care of all those furry little creatures."

Margo wanted to decline the invitation, but she wasn't about to let this city woman think she'd been intimidated. Miss Humphreys probably planned to show up every woman invited.

"Sure," Rebel said tightly. "I think a little party's in order. I'll get on the phone first thing—see if I can round up some folks." His eyes rested on Margo. "You'll come, won't you?"

"I guess I can come."

"Bring your aunt," Rebel added. "Maybe your grandfather will come along too this time."

And pigs fly! Margo thought without amusement.

Roxanne fluttered a hand upward, her mandarin-red fingernails glistening in the late afternoon sun. "And bring your husband." She raised a well-arched eyebrow. "I'd like to meet him." Her crimson lips turned up in a smile but her dark eyes, as black as jet beads, remained as cold as a winter frost.

"I'm not married," Margo said simply.

"Ohh!" Roxanne lengthened the word in a long breath.

Rebel shot her an irritated look. "We can talk about

the party later, Roxanne." Then he said to Margo, "Let's go see ol' Henry."

Roxanne grimaced when they turned to walk on together. Rebel's expression was difficult to read. Yet Margo had the feeling he didn't enjoy the little exchange any more than she had.

Inside the stables, they went directly to the ailing horse's stall. Clean hay had been scattered on the floor. The horse didn't raise his head this time.

Rebel's mouth tightened. He ran his hand over the horse's forelock. "Poor guy."

Ed came up behind them. "Ol' Henry looked pretty peaked yesterday but nothing like this. Miguel came over to the bunkhouse to fetch me."

Rebel's gaze pleaded with Margo to do something, making her feel even more downhearted.

"It's time," she said quietly, meeting his helpless eyes. "There's nothing else to be done for him."

Rebel cleared his throat. "I know you're right but it doesn't make it any easier."

A lump formed in Margo's throat too. "Tomorrow, then?" The look on Rebel's face told her how bad he felt. She reached out to touch his arm.

"Tomorrow," he murmured, eyes filled with torment. "We'll haul him up to the foothills for burial."

With Roxanne settled in one of the guest bedrooms after her long trip, Rebel came downstairs and poured himself a stiff shot of brandy. Usually he didn't drink much but the thought of losing Henry turned his stomach into knots. The horse had been a fine companion in its prime. Only a year ago the gelding could run across the desert as though he had wings.

Rebel took a sip of the brandy and swallowed. The fiery liquid burned his throat. He was furious with Roxanne, and in no mood for the pointless party she had manipulated him into giving. She'd get a king-size shock when he escorted her into the Spanish Spur Tavern. He wanted her to find out pronto just how much his lifestyle had changed.

Roxanne's sudden appearance brought back painful memories. What really brought her to California? She never did anything without an ulterior motive. Although he thought he loved her once, all that had changed long ago. In the beginning she seemed so different from the Southern women with whom he'd grown up, far more sophisticated and worldly. But as soon as he discovered her father's offer of a partnership in his prestigious law firm was predicated on his marriage to Roxanne, he saw the handwriting on the wall. Rebel would be forever under her domineering father's thumb. He began to notice other things he wasn't keen on, her temper and self-absorption. What a fool he'd been.

On the day he learned he'd inherited the Circle G, he grabbed a cab and hurried over to Roxanne's Park Avenue apartment. At first she seemed excited, telling him it would be a wonderful place for them to vacation during New York's cold winters. But when he told her he intended to settle out West, she shrieked and quickly informed him she could never live away from the convenience of New York City.

"We couldn't attend concerts at Carnegie Hall or Radio City. And all the best plays open here," she had cried. "Where would I get my hair and nails done—my massages?"

Roxanne had pleaded with Rebel to stay in New

York, but he stuck to his guns, actually relieved by the breakup. And now here she was messing up his chances with Margo Fitzgerald, a woman totally opposite from her. On top of everything else, ol' Henry was at death's door. Roxanne would think his concern for the horse quaint. Margo, however, understood.

Rebel flopped into a chair, placing his feet on an ottoman. He had been shocked when Margo accused him of being engaged, wondering where she'd gotten that outdated information. No, things couldn't be worse. He agonized over how to convince her he wasn't an insincere lout. Knowing Roxanne as he did, he figured she would stoop at nothing to make him look bad if she suspected he was interested in the lady vet.

Maybe the party was a good idea, after all. At least he would have others around to entertain her.

In a little while Roxanne descended the spiral staircase wearing a black designer gown. The gown looked about as out of place on his ranch as a Halston creation.

"Darling, it's so good to see you," she murmured, throwing her arms around his neck and giving him a kiss.

Unsmiling, he pulled her arms down.

Chapter Eleven

Margo had just come in from delivering a healthy foal and her spirits were high. She gave Hattie a hug and poured herself a cup of coffee, taking a seat at the kitchen table. "Birth is such a magical thing," she said. "You should have seen the foal get up on those spindly legs."

"Oh! I just remembered something." Hattie hurried to a large box by the back door and picked it up. "It came this afternoon—from that shop in the mall. What did you buy?"

Margo shook her head. "I didn't buy anything. It's a mistake. I'll call UPS and have them return it."

Curious, Hattie said, "It's got your name on it, missy. Open it and let's see."

Reluctantly, Margo took the knife Hattie handed her and cut the tape, then pulled back the flaps. Removing the tissue paper, she was surprised to see an attractive straw cowgirl hat.

"Well, I'll be," Hattie said, abuzz. "It's pretty fancy.

Must be made out of that Panama straw, the kind you can't crush."

Margo's mouth flew open. She lifted it out of the box, admiring the blue feathered band. A card lay on the bottom of the box. Hesitant, she opened it with trembling fingers, recalling what Rebel had said on the cattle roundup about buying her a new hat. Sure enough, his name was on the gift card.

Hattie snatched the card from Margo and scanned it. "Rebel sent you this expensive hat? What's this all about?"

Shock waves shot through Margo. "I don't know where to begin."

"At the beginning." Hattie grinned, taking a seat at the table opposite her.

"When I went on that roundup, you know, the one I told you about? Rebel was there, too. Rouge went down in a prairie-dog hole and I got thrown. I landed on my hat."

"You didn't tell me."

"It was nothing. He kiddingly said he wanted to buy me a hat. Well, I guess he's gone and done it."

"Isn't that nice. Southerners are such gentlemen. Why don't you bake him a batch of cookies or maybe a cake?" Hattie smirked.

Margo scowled. "I can't keep this! And I'm not baking cookies."

Hattie's brows sprang together. "What's gotten into you, child? The man's done you a favor. Why are you acting all riled up? It's not like you."

How could Margo confide everything to her aunt now? "I. . . . well . . ."

Hattie pointed her finger at Margo. "You keep that hat, hear? He went to a lot of trouble. Men usually hate to shop."

"Oh, all right. But just the same, I think it's a mistake to keep it."

"I'm sure no strings are attached. He's too fine a man for that."

"Hmm." Margo took the hat and left Hattie alone in the kitchen. So Rebel wasn't buying the present for his ex-fiancée after all. *What an idiot you are!*

Rebel had hurriedly arranged the party for Roxanne. He came downstairs early. Glancing at himself in the mirror, he glowered. Then he adjusted a turquoise bolo tie around the neck of his black western-style shirt. This wasn't a night he looked forward to. At the moment Roxanne lingered upstairs primping. When he had passed by the open door of the guest room a whiff of her expensive perfume brought back an unpleasant reminder of their former relationship. She'd emerge soon enough, probably in a knockout gown with a designer label and a price tag to match, ready to impress the country folks. He had told her most people dressed casually at the tavern. But when did Roxanne ever dress down?

He poured himself a stiff brandy and slumped down at a small table with a chess board on top. A few days ago he'd set out the game with the intention of challenging Ed, Too bad they weren't playing now. But nothing was happening as he had anticipated—ol' Henry dying, for an example. That morning, together with Margo and Ed, he buried him on the ranch. Margo brought a bouquet of flowers from her garden—a nice touch.

Rebel fretted. Henry had been a fine horse.

In a little while a rustle on the spiral staircase announced Roxanne. Her feet hardly touched the steps. Her head was held just so, as though she carried two books on top. Sure enough, she was dressed to the teeth all in white.

He pushed back the chair and crossed to her, his boots scraping on the floor. "You look lovely," he said. She smiled. He glanced at his wristwatch. "Ed should be bringing the car around about now. It's time we were going." Her slender arms came up to wrap around his neck, but he said calmly, "Don't do that."

Her arms fell beside her like a lifeless mannequin's. "You don't mind a friendly kiss?"

He didn't respond.

Her eyebrows arched in that derisive way he was so familiar with, as she turned to inspect her lips in the mirror over the fireplace. He caught her examining his western-style clothes through the reflection in the mirror.

She turned back to him. "Do you like my dress? I chose it especially for you." Her hands slid over the fabric.

"Sure. Real nice." The truth was, she looked positively elegant in her backless dress. She'd done something funny to her hair, making it look even more sophisticated. Large diamond earrings dangled from her earlobes, and an emerald the size of his thumbnail hung at her swanlike neck.

"I can't wait to meet your friends," she gushed. She glided purposefully across the floor to the coffee table to retrieve a gold cigarette case she had left there earlier. Her high heels made her lithe body tilt slightly forward. In the old days he would have already been reaching out to her but now he merely stood there, his arms folded.

Roxanne took out a cigarette and placed it between her lips. Rebel lit it. She inhaled deeply, her eyes traveling over him, and her mouth turned up slightly. "Don't you think you're carrying this Western thing a trifle far? One would think you were the Marlboro Man, darling." She tossed him a jeering smile.

"Hmm," he muttered. "Hadn't thought about it." Pure determination kept his irritation under wraps. "You, however, are still as beautiful as I remembered."

He knew he had caught Roxanne off guard, and for a moment she didn't speak, then she brightened. "And you're still my gallant Rebel."

The hungry look in her eyes made him brace himself when she moved a step closer to slip her arms under his. Her flaming lips were already puckered like a ripe persimmon, but to his relief, the doorbell rang. Rebel made a fast retreat to the door, gratefully expelling his breath in relief.

Ed stood there, looking as though he had made a concerted effort to be dapper—freshly shaved, mustache combed, hair slicked back, and wearing a new plaid shirt. The tops of his boots shone like a pond after a spring rain.

"Come on in, Ed." Rebel held the door open for him. "We're ready."

"The car's out front." The foreman gave Roxanne a polite nod and touched the brim of his hat, as she stood across the room smoking. "Ma'am."

She barely acknowledged him, a corner of her mouth lifting. Rebel hoped she'd be more polite to his guests.

They left the house. Ed opened a back door for Roxanne, then started to slide into the driver's seat.

Rebel said, "I'll drive."

"You sure?" Ed looked doubtful.

Rebel nodded. He figured his foreman was planning to play the chauffeur role, but Rebel had no intention of letting him tonight. Ed was his guest, and that meant Rebel would do the driving.

Ed closed the back door for Roxanne, then hopped into the passenger seat. Rebel took off.

The Spanish Spur lay only a few miles away on the outskirts of Indio. When Rebel swung into the parking lot, his heart pounded with anxiety when he didn't see Margo's Cherokee. Did she change her mind about coming? He had heard the Fitzgeralds were in serious financial trouble, and he itched to lend a hand.

However, he didn't know how to broach the subject to Margo. She was a proud one.

He parked and eased out from behind the wheel as Ed ran around to open the door for Roxanne. She put out a well-curved leg without thanking him. Rebel grinned. Good old Ed—determined to be courteous.

Inside the tavern they stood for a moment to let their eyes adjust to the semidarkness. Yellowish light bulbs behind the bar and the red neon signs welcomed them to a world where guests discarded peanut shells on the floor. Roxanne looked askance at the ceiling where antlers, cowboy chaps, business cards, and pieces of discarded clothing hung. In a corner of the large room, two musicians in battered cowboy hats strummed a Garth Brooks song on twangy electric guitars. A third man pounded a synthesizer keyboard and sang with gusto. Roxanne attempted a weak smile before clapping her palms over her ears to protest the blaring music. Rebel raised his brows. The Spanish Spur had a reputation for being rough-and-tumble. He was sure she had never been in a place like it in her life—and never would again.

A hostess dressed in a short leather skirt and T-shirt flashed Rebel a smile. "I've got your table ready, hon," she said. "Follow me."

She led them through a group of line-dancers to the corner farthest from the band. Rebel thanked her and pulled out a seat for Roxanne at the large round table. He didn't miss the numerous stares his former fiancée received. Roxanne's nose twisted into an odd shape. She apparently found the musty smells of the place offensive. Well, she wanted to get a taste of the West, and this was it.

Against his better judgment, Rebel had had another talk with Michael. He didn't like asking him to Roxanne's party after he'd punched him, but he needed someone smooth enough to entertain her while he attempted to make up with Margo. Michael had agreed to let bygones be bygones. But to Rebel's consternation, Michael brought Julie. A smudged imprint of lipstick was on his cheek and his nose was still swollen, the circles under his eyes discolored. After the introductions Michael dropped into the chair on the other side of Roxanne, apparently impressed by her beauty.

Margo and Hattie arrived late. Rebel breathed a sigh of relief. He was afraid she might not show. With Hattie, she made her way around the other tables to reach his party. His heart beat in an unnatural rhythm. She looked gorgeous, if distant, a shadow over her eyes. He extended a hand to the women.

"Welcome. Glad you both could come." He leaned over and brushed a welcoming kiss across Margo's temple, catching the scent of her sweet natural essence. She stiffened.

"Thanks for asking us," she said, her tone noncommittal.

Hattie murmured a thanks too.

Julie waved. "Hey, girlfriend."

Margo answered in kind, and greeted everyone around the table. She started to take the chair next to Julie, but Rebel put out a hand to stop her.

"I saved you a seat right here." He pulled out the chair beside him before she could protest.

Roxanne, on the opposite side, leaned forward and scrutinized Margo's casual clothes. Her lips curled up in a smile but her eyes remained somber.

"Roxanne, you remember Margo Fitzgerald, my vet," Rebel said. "This is her Aunt Hattie."

"How nice to meet you," Roxanne said.

Hattie replied, "Likewise," and set her gaze on Ed. He pulled out a chair for her, grinning broadly.

Roxanne entwined her arm positively with Rebel's when he sat back down, and unleashed a captivating smile intended only for him.

He caught Margo's frown. Apparently Roxanne wanted everyone present to think they were still engaged. Proving it untrue wouldn't be easy for Rebel.

Margo looked particularly attractive in an ankle-length suede skirt. Her blouse was the color of ripe apricots. It accented her cinnamon-tinted eyes. She had let down her hair. It fanned around her lovely shoulders, making him want to reach out to run his fingers through its shimmering ginger waves. A strand of turquoise and silver beads warmed the delicate flesh at her throat.

Hattie's amused chuckle pulled him from his reverie. He hardly recognized the woman when she came in. Her new short, curly hairstyle made her appear more youthful. Ed's eyes were practically falling out of his head, and his mouth formed an O each time she spoke. Was Ed smitten or what? Rebel forced a laugh down.

Ed said, "Come on, Hattie. Let's you and me dance before that little band winds down."

Hattie wasted no time getting to her feet. Taking his hand, she grinned. "I'm ready."

Michael leaned over Margo and spoke to her about running into a door. Rebel smoldered. Surely the man understood he was to stay away from her from now on.

"I'm still waiting for your call," Michael said.

Did he want another fist in the nose? Rebel fumed. He didn't hear her reply because another couple, the Martins, joined their table. Chad Martin's partner, Les Arden, had tagged along. They were Rebel's farm agents. Rebel introduced them to Roxanne. They all gathered around the table and broke into conversations.

Before Rebel realized it, Michael was sitting next to Margo, and the developer had her full attention. Rebel didn't like the direction the evening was taking. He, not Michael, should be talking to Margo. His plans were fizzling faster than cheap champagne. Why wasn't Michael overwhelming Roxanne? Worse, Margo was laughing at one of his inane jokes.

Michael went on in his jovial way, his rapid-fire jokes clearly amusing everyone. Rebel asked Roxanne to dance, just to be polite. Even she seemed reluctant to miss the man's next witticism. Rebel covered his irritation with a carefully controlled reserve.

By the time they came back to the table, a waitress had brought pitchers of ice tea and bowls of tortilla chips and salsa. Rebel kept an eye on Margo and Michael, who were now dancing. Michael held her so close Rebel's blood pressure escalated. At first he thought he had detected a certain coolness in Margo's attitude toward his golfing chum, but he must have been wrong. She was laughing and having a good time.

When they finally returned, Margo's face looked flushed. Michael hardly sat down before launching into another joke, this one about Tarzan. Rebel rubbed his eyes and studied the ceiling.

To his dismay, Michael continued to show only a passing interest in Roxanne. Rebel tried to put a good face on it and play the congenial host, but all he wanted was to get Margo alone.

"Dance?" he asked her, rising to his feet and holding out a hand.

Margo smiled none too warmly but rose, ignoring his outstretched hand. "Sure, Rebel."

He took it anyway. The touch of Rebel's hand on hers created a storm in Margo's heart that she fought very hard to control. She looked steadily into his face while her lips parted. "Your girlfriend seems to be enjoying herself."

"She's not my girlfriend."

"Your fiancée, then."

"Stop it, Margo."

Tiny crow's-feet at the corners of his eyes crinkled into a frown. His big hand squeezed her fingers gently, but with complete authority, as he guided her on the dance floor.

"You look beautiful tonight," he said, his voice husky. "And you know I'm nuts about you."

His endearing words caused her breath to catch in her throat. "Rebel. I don't know what to say."

"Stash a bit of courage in your pocket and admit you care for me," he said, his eyes hooded.

She couldn't speak. He drew her closer, his palm increasing its pressure on the small of her back. Taking her hand protectively, he cupped it to his chest like something precious. At that moment he won over her heart, making her want to stay in his arms forever. She let her lashes sweep down, then opened her eyes to lock with his. "Thanks for the hat. It was a real surprise."

"Glad you like it." Then he chided her. "Margo, darling, you've been keeping your distance, but it won't work. You must realize that." He searched her face, holding her body so close she could hardly breath.

"We need to talk," she said. "But how can I believe you when Roxanne is hanging all over you?"

"It's all show. Curse your stubbornness," he said, kissing her throat. "I don't want to dance with anyone but you tonight. Can't you see that? Let's run away. They don't need us."

She shook her head, laughing, then immediately did an about face and turned serious. "You danced with Roxanne twice before you asked me!"

"You were hanging on to Michael's every word like he was giving away free cotton candy!"

Margo had to laugh at his ridiculous remark. "You were spying on me. I saw you."

Rebel grinned. "And you were trying to make me jealous. Well, it worked."

They moved in sync to the rhythm of the country-western music. He twirled her away from him and brought her back in a fluid movement, as though they were the only dancers on the floor. His mesmerizing lapis-blue eyes held her gaze, refusing to let it drift away. He pressed his lips to hers, and she yearned to be alone with him in some secluded place. Delicious, vivid images flooded her thoughts.

When the dance ended, Rebel didn't let Margo go. "I'm going to keep you right here in my arms all night, darling, until you agree to see me again."

"Mmm, that would be lovely." How could she go on denying she cared for him?

The music resumed. If he could hold her here so tenderly, surely he didn't have any feelings left for Roxanne, she told herself.

Gathering her courage, Margo said in a hushed tone, "Rebel, I'm sorry I didn't believe you—about Roxanne, I mean. And I do care for you." She stared at his gentle, steady gaze and felt him become less tense.

"I've been waiting to hear those priceless words all evening."

She rested her cheek against the curve of his throat and he leaned down to stroke the top of her ear with his lips. The light stubble of his beard was reassuringly masculine.

"You smell so good," he said.

She knew her eyes sparked, revealing her feelings. "You too."

His warm breath caressed her, as his lips moved across her cheekbone. "I'm crazy about you—have been since the first time I met you. Margo, darling, there mustn't be any doubts between us, ever."

"I want to believe that, Rebel."

The music ended and the musicians laid their instruments down for a break, forcing Rebel to release her. Hand in hand, they strolled back to the table, Margo now dreamy-eyed. Michael had his arm around Roxanne's shoulders. Margo wondered if Julie was jealous, but her friend was chatting up a storm with Les Arden, apparently completely oblivious. Roxanne looked up and gave Rebel a chilly stare, then turned back to Michael and blew a puff of cigarette smoke in his face.

She said, "There's simply no place in the world like New York City in the spring. You must give me a call next time you're in town, Michael—providing I'm still there, of course." She threw him a fetching grin and leaned forward.

Julie turned. "I've been to New York too," she said, glancing around the table for emphasis. "It was dirty, terribly crowded, and I could hardly draw a decent, unpolluted breath!"

Roxanne's classic features shifted from a practiced smile to an open glare. "Fortunately, I don't live in *that* part of the city!" She dismissed Julie as though her opinion was of no importance and focused on Margo. "Rebel tells me you saved a polo pony when it wandered onto his ranch. Too bad you couldn't save his horse as well." She drew another cigarette out of the gold case and snapped it shut with a practiced display of ostentation. Michael jumped up to light it for her, almost tripping over Julie's legs, ending by spilling soda in her lap.

Julie jumped up as well. "You idiot!" She took off in a huff, heading for the ladies room.

Margo couldn't let Roxanne's remark about ol' Henry go unchallenged, deeply sorry she couldn't save him. "I wish I could have restored him to good health, but I'm afraid the horse's problems were due to the aging process."

Rebel shot a glare at Roxanne before turning to Margo. "No need to apologize."

Julie returned from the ladies room and grabbed Les's hand. "Dance with me."

"Okay, beautiful," he said. A tall man, he lumbered to his feet and stretched out his arms.

The waitress appeared with heaping platters of aromatic tacos, enchiladas, and tamales. The group fell silent, except for oohing and aahing over the mouth-watering Mexican dishes.

However, after taking a taste or two, Roxanne twisted slightly in her chair and pushed her plate away. "I'm looking forward to seeing your grand ranch tomorrow, Rebel, darling," she said in a voice that could charm a cobra.

Noticing she wasn't eating, he frowned. What was she expecting, paella?

"We'll leave at seven," he said dryly. He'd make quick work of it, knowing she had only a bare-bones interest.

Her eyes widened. "Seven! Isn't that rather early? You know I'm never up before eleven."

A moment of dead silence hung in the air. Then Hattie snorted. "Humph!" She cocked an inquisitorial eyebrow at the woman. "I've got half my work done by then."

Rebel sighed dispassionately at Roxanne's remark about his knowing her sleep patterns, and glanced over at Margo. She stared straight ahead. He tried to come up with something appropriate to say. Knowing himself, he figured he'd come up with a beaut in the wee hours of the night. Margo was now studying him with her guileless eyes. Her generous lips made him forget what he was about to say when she smiled. He smiled back. The tension across his forehead relaxed a little, but he knew it was going to be a long night.

The room grew noisier as the band took up their instruments. Over in the corner Rebel spotted a group of men arguing. He figured there'd be trouble before long. It was time to wrap up the party.

Ed interrupted his thoughts when he began to tell a story. "Had a horse that lived to be twenty," he jovially told the group. "Named him Miser when he was a colt 'cause he was always stealing his stable-mate's oats."

Hattie howled. The others chuckled, even though what he said wasn't very funny and didn't come up to Michael's witticisms. Rebel turned to speak to Margo, catching her biting into a taco. Some of the juice spilled on her hand and she wiped it off. "When you're finished, let's dance."

She nodded, embarrassed. "Maybe I need a bib. I'm so messy."

Rebel reached out, handing her another napkin. "You're awfully pretty," he murmured.

Roxanne toyed with the edge of her own napkin and glowered. Even though she wasn't looking directly at him, he knew she'd eavesdropped by her delicate cough. She started talking about her New York friends and how they planned to vacation in Virginia during the summer.

"I've always been positively dazzled by country life, although I've experienced little of it," she hurried on. "I have friends who own a stud farm near Monticello and we'll all go fox hunting."

The Mexican food congealed on her plate.

Get real! Rebel wanted to say. *You don't know one end of a horse from the other.* But he kept quiet, knowing a gentleman didn't start a quarrel in front of guests. Besides, his relationship with Roxanne lay in the past, not the future.

The band played on, and the keyboard player sang, "All My Exes Live in Texas."

Roxanne got up to dance with Michael, effectively taking her off Rebel's hands. Finally, things were going right. He asked Margo to dance.

At the edge of the dance floor, she moved into his arms. The band switched to the romantic "*Have you ever been lonely, have you ever been blue.*"

His tall, lean body pressed comfortingly against Margo. His unblinking eyes bored into her with heartfelt emotion until she had to look away momentarily to catch her breath. The strong beat of his heart made her own speed up. Rebel had lit a spark inside her that released emotions she had never experienced.

When the song ended, he murmured, "It's nice to relax with you, Margo. When can I see you again?"

"Soon," she replied, her voice a whisper.

When they came back to the table, fingers entwined, Roxanne was sitting Stiffly alone. She jumped up and stood as straight as Queen Elizabeth addressing her subjects. She threw her napkin on the table and scowled at Rebel, ignoring Margo. Red splotches circled her cheeks.

"Rebel Gentry, I cannot believe how you've changed, chasing this woman all evening like a lovesick puppy!

Well, you can take me back to the ranch! I'm going home tomorrow! I detest this horrid, smelly place! It's certainly not the Tavern-On-The-Green, like I expected! And, let me tell you, I've never been so utterly humiliated—sitting here all alone like some sort of castoff!"

Rebel, who had just sat down, nearly choked. Getting his breath, he said politely, "I'm sorry you're not having a good time, Roxanne. Where did everyone go?"

"How am I supposed to know? They're dancing, I guess." Fuming, she plopped back down and picked up a cigarette, stuffing it in her mouth with a shaky hand.

Michael came back in time to catch the action and tossed Rebel a bemused grin behind Roxanne's back. He had been dancing with Julie.

The other guests returned before the dust settled. Roxanne sniffed, her nose high. They stared first at her, then at Margo. Roxanne's face was crimson. Margo's had gone white. Rebel was trying to figure out what he ought to say to smooth things over when he saw a fight start over in the corner.

"Let's get out of here, folks, before bottles start flying."

He hurriedly hustled them outside before it could escalate, coming back only long enough to pay the tab. The Spanish Spur was warming up, but their own evening had been almost too hot to handle.

In the parking lot Roxanne jerked open the front car door, slamming it shut behind her. Julie turned up her nose at Michael, and after a few hot words of her own, climbed into Les Arden's sports car. Margo and her aunt were the first to pull out of the parking lot. Rebel sighed deeply, threw a quick glance over his shoulder at Ed in the backseat, and shot the Jaguar into reverse. Roxanne would surely have plenty to say once they reached the ranch. He groaned.

Chapter Twelve

When Margo merged into traffic, Hattie said, "Roxanne's a shallow woman. People like that have a driving need for attention. Did you see how highfalutin' she was dressed? Like some model on a Paris runway. And just as skinny."

Rebel said he didn't care for Roxanne anymore, and when they were together Margo believed him. Yet once they were apart, doubts crept back to vex her.

Hattie threw her a sidelong glance. "Admit it, you ninny, Rebel's crazy about you, and you about him. Don't worry about that woman. Sure, she'd like to get her hooks in him again, but he's not buying it."

Margo's mouth softened. "Oh, Hattie, life can certainly get complicated. I was so embarrassed when she said those things."

Hattie shook her head. "I saw the look in Rebel's eyes when he danced with you, hon. I'm not blind, you know. Love was written smack all over his face."

Margo's interest heightened. "Really? Do you think so?"

"It was love, all right."

Two days later Margo met Rebel for lunch at the La Quinta Country Club restaurant. She wore the new hat.

He grinned, admiring the way she had the new hat pulled low, making her eyes seem wonderfully mysterious. "Looks just right on you."

"You're a thoughtful man," she said, smiling. "Thanks again."

"If you fall off your horse on that one, I'll buy you another."

Margo chuckled. "That's a hard way to get a new hat. I might break my neck next time."

"Maybe you need a hard hat," he teased. "Let's hope you never take another tumble, unless it's into my arms."

"I wouldn't mind that." She smiled, although an underlying anxiety swept through her—but not because of him. An hour earlier she had been at the bank receiving the bad news—definitely no loan. She thought about telling Rebel but didn't want to cloud their fresh understanding with her problems.

"You're only nibbling your salad," he said. "Something wrong with it? We'll send it back." He looked around for the waiter.

"No, it's fine." She took a sip of sparkling water, wanting to change the subject. "I understand you're expecting a bumper crop of grapes this summer."

He grinned. "Yeah. That extra rainfall this spring came just at the right time. I'm also about ready to begin my Arabian stud farm—with your help, that is."

Her interest perked up immediately. "Great. I think that's such a good idea. I've compiled some information for you, if you're interested."

"Of course I am. I've been thinking about it for some time. Arabians are great desert horses. I've got plenty of room in my stables, although I might need to expand later on. Would you consider helping me pick out a stallion and a few brood mares? You did a fine job with Jake."

Margo finished the last drop of sparkling water. "Of course. It's terribly exciting—raising Arabians!"

Rebel paid the bill and they strolled out to the parking lot, admiring the blanket of pansies and petunias planted in the gardens around the hotel grounds. He opened the car door for her. She liked his courtly manners, so different from most men she knew.

She slid in, and he eased himself into the driver's seat, but he didn't turn on the ignition right away. "Can we talk a minute?" he asked. "Something's bothering you, Margo. What's the problem? Still mad at me? Roxanne's gone—and forever."

"Oh, no." She bit the inside of her lower lip. "It's nothing, really." *You liar,* she told herself with a touch of contempt. Why couldn't she level with him? After all, this was a man she cared deeply about.

"Share it with me, now! I can't stand this lack of communication—your unwillingness to trust me."

"I do trust you!" She couldn't keep her voice steady.

"Yeah, I can see how much you trust me." He laughed without humor. "Sometimes you seem to slip away from me, Margo. C'mon, tell me what's bothering you or we'll sit here all afternoon."

She took a deep breath, then let it out. "I . . . we . . .

oh, it's everything! It's Grandpa. He's got Alzheimer's! It's the taxes! We're about to lose our ranch, I'm afraid." A lone tear escaped down her cheek.

Rebel wiped it away and cradled her in his arms, brushing a wisp of hair from her forehead. She took out a tissue and blew her nose. He didn't speak, letting her pour out all the pent-up hurt and frustration she had bottled up.

When she quieted, he murmured, "The taxes are due in six days, Margo."

Rebel's remark brought on a barrage of tears, wetting the shoulder of his shirt, but he didn't care. His heart went out to her. If money was what she needed, he had plenty to share.

"I tried to get a loan," she stammered. "But they turned me down flat this morning. Grandpa's had that ranch for fifty years and we've always paid our debts."

He kissed her wet cheek. "I'll give you the money." He'd give her anything she asked for.

She stiffened, wiggling out of his arms. "Oh, no! I could never take charity. My grandfather wouldn't hear of it, either. Why, the Fitzgeralds lived in a tent their first year here in the valley. We've always taken care of ourselves. You don't think I'm telling you all this to make you feel sorry for us?"

"Hush now," he said, pulling her back into the protection of his arms. "I'll loan you the money, if that's the way it has to be."

She pulled free again. "No, I'd never let you do that. It would compromise us, don't you see? It would put our relationship in a dreadful position. What if I couldn't pay you back?"

"Oh, Margo! You can be so darn stubborn!" But he

realized arguing would not end their impasse. He'd have to come up with a better solution to satisfy this beautiful, independent woman. His fingers gently kneaded her back muscles as she laid her head on his shoulder. "We'll think of something, darling."

Later, when Margo closed the clinic, she drove home, depressed. Hattie wasn't in the kitchen. She wandered around and grabbed a pear off the bowl on the table. Thinking how to phrase the bad news to her aunt and her grandfather, she saw a white cake with buttercream frosting on the counter. Just as she was about to stick a finger on the side for a secret taste, Hattie came in.

"Keep your fingers off that cake, missy! That's for Ed."

Margo drew it back as though Hattie had slapped it. "Okay, okay!"

Hattie's face split into a wide grin as she thrust a ringless left hand under Margo's nose. "I'm engaged, hon!" she said, beaming. "I'll have a ring soon."

Margo's mouth flew open with a jumble of words she couldn't articulate. "Engaged?"

"Surprise!" Hattie laughed, her eyes filled with joy. "You look like you'd swallowed a minnow. Ed and I are going into town tomorrow to pick out a ring. I'm just thrilled to death! I think I'd like a big pearl. What do you think? Diamonds are too fussy for me."

"Oh, a shiny pearl would be grand," Margo agreed. "So you're getting married? Surprise isn't the word for it! Why, I'm surprised right down to my boots straps. But I couldn't be happier for you."

They exchanged hugs. Then, after giving it a little

more thought, Margo cocked her head. "Hattie, are you sure? You hardly know Ed."

"Of course I'm sure," her aunt insisted. "Ed and I don't have time to waste like you young people. Neither of us are spring chickens. Besides, he's crazy about me—said so at Rebel's party. And I think he's pretty special too."

Margo kissed Hattie's cheek. "Oh, I'm so happy for you."

Hattie leaned back against a kitchen cabinet. "There's just one complication—Daddy! I haven't told him yet. You know how he can be such an old warthog these days. Well, I didn't want to get his dander up—start him on one of his tirades. Since Ed works for the Circle G, he'll probably throw a conniption."

"But you have to tell him."

"That's where I need your help, hon." Hattie turned around and carefully dropped a maraschino cherry in the center of the cake.

Margo felt disaster inching toward her. "My help? What can I do?"

"Hmm. I was thinking about that very thing when I saw you, and I've decided to have a brunch after Mass on Sunday. Just our family, the priest, and Ed and Rebel—sort of being neighborly-like. That's what I'll tell Daddy, although he won't like it. After all, Rebel's invited Daddy over, even if he refused to go. With Father Mark here, Daddy can't object too much, can he? Then, just after we take our seats at the table, you stand up and give a toast announcing our engagement. Great idea—yes?"

"Me? Why, Grandpa'll spit fire for sure if you do it suddenly like that."

"No, he won't. Don't you see? If I tell him ahead of time he might decide to sulk in his room all during the meal. Besides, with the priest here he'll be afraid to act up."

"I don't know." Margo felt the pain in her shoulder return. She could just see her grandfather throwing a king-size tantrum.

"It's not like I'm sixteen!" Hattie sulked. "He ought to be glad to see his daughter finally married."

"Yes, that's true. But somehow he still sees us both as young girls."

"Besides, Daddy's happy as a lark right now. He came out here not more than twenty minutes ago. Got a call from Mr. Carlton. He found a buyer for our alfalfa. Isn't that terrific? Like a last-minute reprieve."

Margo clutched her and they whooped and waltzed around the kitchen.

"I can't believe it," she said.

"Ought to take care of the taxes and pay for the wedding, by golly. I figure this couldn't be a better time to break the news."

Margo clutched Hattie to her bosom. "I'll do it, but only because I can't see any other way."

Hattie laughed.

"When will the wedding take place?"

"Next month before the heat sets in. Father Mark's agreed to waive the banns. We'll have the reception right out there in the garden. I'm inviting everyone in the valley we know."

"Wonderful! It'll be perfect—just perfect."

"You'll be my maiden of honor, of course. Ed's planning to ask Rebel to stand up for him."

"This is all so incredible," Margo said, grabbing her

aunt's hands and squeezing. "You're getting married and we'll be able to pay the taxes. Wheeee!"

Then lowering her gaze, Hattie said, "I'm sorry you thought Rebel was engaged. But I had no idea you cared for him."

Margo dropped her hands. "You said his fiancée was coming, remember?"

"Well, I said no such thing! Where'd you get such a notion? I said pure and simple that his ex-fiancée was coming."

Margo started to argue but changed her mind. Hattie's good news had lifted her spirits.

"Maybe there'll be two weddings." Hattie gave her a sly grin. "Want to hear what happened after the party?"

"At Rebel's? No—I mean yes, of course I do."

"Thought so." Hattie's pupils dilated. "Sofia told Ed that a passel of fireworks went off shortly after they got home from the Spanish Spur. The housekeeper was still in the kitchen doing some last-minute things. Well, she said you could hear Rebel and that Roxanne sparring like two roosters."

"What happened?"

"He gave her a good tongue-lashing."

When Hattie paused for effect, Margo said, "Go on, don't stop now."

"Roxanne sent a lot of high-pitched screams vibrating through the house, practically rattling dishes on the shelves. The woman accused him of everything in the book, including wooing you."

"What else did she say about me?" She felt herself color as she sat down heavily on a kitchen chair. "Oh, the nerve of that . . . witch of a woman!"

Hattie nodded. She wiped away a trickle of perspiration on her forehead. "It's hotter than a Dutch oven in here after baking that cake. Let's go out in the garden."

Margo followed her aunt and they sat down on the lawn swing. She breathed deeply in the late afternoon sunshine, needing to think all these revelations through.

"You didn't tell me what else Roxanne said."

"She called us all hillbillies."

"The nerve of her!"

"She doesn't have a heart," Hattie said, sneering. "Treated Ed like some kind of peasant. 'Do this, do that,' she ordered. About drove him to distraction."

Images of Roxanne flickered across Margo's eyes. "I'm glad she's gone."

Hattie fingered her short hair. "Don't moon over Rebel too much during brunch, hear? I have enough to concern me without you and Daddy acting funny."

"Rebel's proud and arrogant," Margo said thoughtfully. "He might refuse your invitation."

"Not on your life."

Margo smiled. She absently touched her lower lip and stared at the little red smudge that came off on her finger. Makeup wasn't something she was used to wearing, but lately she had wanted to look her best.

She wiped it off. "You haven't told me who made the offer on the alfalfa crop."

"Don't know. Daddy just said Mr. Carlton got an excellent offer and he's accepted it. I imagine a letter will arrive with the particulars in a day or two."

Margo smiled. "At least we can thumb our noses at those bankers now."

"Things somehow always work out."

Hattie stretched and kicked off her sandals, her feet splayed on the grass.

"Weddings are so special," she said. "It's a statement to the world that you belong to each other."

Grandpa Fitz's voice boomed in high decibels from the kitchen door. "Margo, you're wanted on the phone."

"Coming, Grandpa," she called, thinking it might be Rebel.

However, it was only Dr. Thornsey. After she hung up, she sauntered through the house, appraising it as a stranger might do. Except for being clean, the shabby furniture was hardly ready for guests. The once brightly patterned chintz sofa and love seat in the living room had faded and its springs sagged. Rebel Gentry would be coming to the house for the first time, and she wanted everything to be just right.

Chapter Thirteen

After Mass on Sunday the Fitzgeralds rove home with tension bouncing off the walls of the vehicle like lightning rods. Margo pulled to a halt in the driveway and Grandpa Fitz hopped out, giving the door a fling.

"It beats me why you invited those men, it does. Don't you know Mr. Gentry's only coming over here to spy on us?" He loosened his tie with his ham of a hand. "Saints preserve us! Why did you make me wear this confounded thing? I can't see any good reason for dressing up."

"Behave yourself, Daddy," Hattie warned, "or I'll lock you in the storeroom."

"You wouldn't!" Grandpa Fitz exploded.

"Oh, wouldn't I!" Hattie growled.

Margo sighed heavily. Angst was part of her grandfather's nature, along with the need to out-shout everyone else.

"Come on, you two," she begged. "Father Mark can't be far behind us. Do you want him to think he's not welcome? Your faces are both flushed."

Grandpa Fitz clamped his jaw tighter than a rich man's wall safe and unlocked the front door, refusing to look at either of them. Inside, he removed his tie and flung it on the back of an overstuffed chair, along with his suit coat. Hattie glared, picked them up as though he had left a wet dishcloth there, and marched out of the room mumbling to herself. Grandpa had won his point about the tie and no amount of arguing would make him put it back on. As for the suit coat—they could forget it.

He slumped down heavily in his recliner, stretched out his arthritic knees, and took his pipe off the side table, filling it from a pouch of aromatic tobacco. Cupping his hand, he lit a match and watched as it flared up among the shredded leaves, then puffed furiously. His Irish setter came in and laid beside his chair.

"Maybe we should put him out for a while, since we're having company," Margo said hopefully. "He sheds this time of year."

"Let the poor dog alone." Then he leaned forward expectantly. "The mail! Did you read yesterday's mail, granddaughter?"

"No, I thought you did. Hattie put it on your desk."

He muttered crossly and lumbered out of the chair, groaning. "I'm expecting an important letter from Mr. Carlton, I am. Counted on you to keep tabs on it. Do I have to do everything around here myself?"

"I'll go get it," Margo offered.

He shook his head, his jowls shaking. "Now that I'm up, I'll get it myself."

Margo watched him toddle out of the room and down the hall, smoke streaming behind him, and she sighed.

The guests would arrive in a matter of minutes. She

hurried through the dining room, where the seldom-used table had been set earlier with a white tablecloth and a centerpiece of flowers from the garden.

When she opened the kitchen door Hattie was bending over a saucepan, stirring its contents. She wore her fanciest Battenburg lace apron.

"Daddy can be so aggravating," she snapped. "I already smell that awful pipe tobacco of his."

"Don't let him get under your skin."

"I know you're right but it isn't easy. This is a very important day for me."

Margo leaned against the refrigerator, going over in her mind the engagement toast she'd stayed awake half the night trying to memorize. This brunch was destined to be an almighty disaster—with a capital D!

"You look lost in thought," Hattie said, maybe an ounce less frazzled. Beads of perspiration had popped out on her forehead.

"It's nothing." Margo didn't want her aunt to know how nervous she herself felt. "I was just wondering what to do next."

Hattie shot her a look. "Go see if Father Mark's gotten here yet. Daddy'll talk his leg off about the old days."

Father Mark had just arrived and had taken a seat on the sofa when Margo came back to the living room.

"Enjoyed the Mass this morning, I did," her grandfather said, standing over the priest, dropping ashes.

"Thank you. I haven't seen you for a while, Mr. Fitzgerald," the priest said, brushing ash off his black trousers.

Grandpa opened his mouth to reply, when he was interrupted by the doorbell's chime. Margo's heart did a somersault. Rebel! She excused herself and rushed to the entrance.

Rebel and Ed stood there, smiling like twins, and handed her identical bouquets of pink carnations.

"Oh, how lovely. Thanks. Come in, won't you?" Margo stacked one bouquet on top of the other in the crook of her arm. She hoped her yellow ankle-length dress looked appropriate for the occasion.

Rebel brushed her cheek with his lips and stood staring at her with a warm, tender gaze. "You look pretty, Margo."

She pushed back a tendril of hair. "Thank you." He looked perfect, dressed in a gray suit and navy blue shirt.

Ed cleared his throat. "That's a mighty pretty dress." His voice held a smile.

"Thanks, Ed. My grandfather is looking forward to meeting both of you," she said, knowing it was a bald-faced lie.

They followed her into the living room. Rebel hurried toward the elderly man with his hand outstretched. "You must be Mr. Fitzgerald. I'm Rebel Gentry, your neighbor," he said. Then he turned and exchanged a handshake with the priest. Ed did the same.

To Margo's surprise her grandfather eyed Rebel with interest, and indicated the seat beside him. "Glad to have you in my house, I am, Mr. Gentry." His face widened into a broad grin, the likes of which she hadn't seen in a long time. "This is Father Mark from our parish. And a fine priest he is, by golly." He proceeded to tell Rebel about the morning's sermon as though he hadn't nodded off a couple of times.

Margo was too shocked to speak for a moment. Then she blurted, "I'll put these flowers in water."

Grandpa jutted his head forward like a turtle, speaking to Rebel and ignoring both Father Mark and Ed.

Would wonders never cease? She hurried into the kitchen. Hattie was poking around in the refrigerator. Margo took down a large green vase from a shelf and turned on the faucet, not knowing quite what to make of the goings-on in the living room. "These are from Rebel and Ed. Aren't they lovely?"

"Very nice. So our guests are here." Hattie closed the refrigerator. "Is Daddy glowering?"

"Will you believe me if I say no?" She waited for her words to register on Hattie, then smiled. "You look particularly pretty in that dress, and I like the way you draped the scarf around your shoulders. So becoming."

"Thanks, hon, but it keeps getting in my way." Hattie's eyes danced, and she reached up to touch the silk scarf. "It's from Ed."

"The man has taste," Margo said. "I'll take our guests a glass of champagne as soon as I finish arranging these flowers. I don't know why my hands feel like they're all thumbs."

"Mm. This pork loin smells good," Hattie said, caught up in her own concerns. "I basted it with my homemade apricot jam." She plugged in an electric knife, and with careful movements, sliced thick slabs of juicy meat. "I hope everything goes just right. You're sure Daddy acted cordial when he met them?"

"Amazingly, yes. Am I dreaming or what?" But she knew the hardest time was yet to come.

Margo picked up the glasses of punch arranged on a

silver platter that they hadn't used in years and carried them into the living room.

"Brunch is nearly ready," she announced, her nerves taut. So far everything appeared mellow. "I brought you a drink while you're waiting." She was struck again by Grandpa Fitz's friendly demeanor. Remarkably, he was going on about a quail hunt he and Rebel's uncle had participated in more than a decade ago.

When the guests had taken a glass and thanked her, Grandpa gave a congenial Irish toast. Margo slipped back to the kitchen to help Hattie put the finishing touches to the meal. She placed the carnations on the buffet in the dining room.

By 1:00 they were seated around the table, with Grandpa Fitz at the head and Father Mark at the other end. Hattie sat beside Ed, her face blooming as pink as the carnations. Margo and Rebel faced them.

Hattie gave her a nudge under the table. Reluctantly, Margo rose. Taking a glass of champagne, she stood up and held it aloft, clearing her throat noisily.

"I . . . I have a surprise announcement to make." She almost lost her voice, and tried not to make eye contact with her grandfather. "My dear Aunt Hattie and Ed, here, are engaged to be married and we all want to wish them a happy future!"

Margo closed her eyes, then opened them wide. At first the room seemed as silent as an empty church hall. Then cheers exploded—and surprisingly, even from her grandfather, who clapped his hands with vigor.

"Well, I'll be a son-of-a-gun! Good! Just fine!" he exclaimed in his deep bass voice. Scrambling to his feet, he gave Hattie a hug and Ed a powerful handshake. "So you finally found yourself a husband, have you, daughter?" He winked.

Hattie kissed his lined cheek, slightly miffed at his blunt remark. The congratulations finally died down.

Still standing bravely, Margo recited the toast she'd prepared. Part of it came from an old greeting card she'd found in a box in the attic. "To a wonderful new beginning, and to hopes and dreams fulfilled, to laughter and shared happiness in all the years to come. And above all, here's to undying love."

"How beautiful!" Hattie cried, grabbing for a tissue in her pocket. "I knew you'd come up with just the right words, hon."

Ed slipped his arm around Hattie's shoulders and they exchanged an emotion-laden kiss. The others chuckled.

"Thanks," Ed murmured to Margo, choking up. "Thanks to you all." He glanced around the table, smiling.

The tender gesture brought tears to Margo's eyes, and she too, fished for a tissue in her pocket. "I'm so happy for you both."

Rebel flashed her a smile. "Well, now that that's over, I have another toast."

Margo collapsed in the dining room chair as all eyes fastened on him.

He held out his glass to her. "Ed and Hattie aren't the only ones announcing their engagement. Margo and I are going to be married as well, if she'll just say yes."

Margo nearly choked. He was proposing?

"Don't disappointment me, darlin'," Rebel said, his eyes glittering. He bent and took her hand.

Overcome, Margo clambered awkwardly to her feet.

In all her life she never dreamed she'd receive so public a proposal.

"Well?" he murmured.

No one moved. The others sat like statues. Grandpa's eyes were as wide as a 45-RPM record.

Margo, listening to her heart for a change, cried, "I . . . yes! I will!"

He embraced her, their lips meeting in a private kiss that made her hunger for more. When they parted, Hattie hugged them both. Ed slapped Rebel on the back. Grandpa said, "This calls for a proper toast!"

He cleared his throat as Hattie poured him a thimbleful of champagne. "First, to my daughter and her intended."

They all tipped their glasses.

"And here's to my granddaughter and her fine man.

"And last of all, here's to Rebel Gentry, who bought our alfalfa crop and saved our hide. To tell you, son, I don't recall what your uncle and I got ourselves so steamed up about all those years ago. Come to think of it, I think it was over who shot the most quail . . . or was it about a huntin' dog? Oh, well."

He tilted his glass and gulped, the others following— all except Margo.

"You bought the alfalfa crop?" she said. Hadn't they discussed Rebel's wanting to help before and she'd declined? She felt her temper rising. Rebel had pulled a fast one.

He must have read her mind, because he leaned closer and murmured tenderly, "I love you, Margo."

"But Rebel—"

"No more talk," Grandpa Fitz interrupted, glowering. "It's done and be thankful."

Everyone talked at once. Then Hattie said, "This food is going to get cold. Let's eat."

" 'Tis a fine day, is it not?" Grandpa Fitz said. "There'll soon be two weddings in this family."

Everyone agreed, then turned their attention to passing bowls and the platter of meat. All except Margo. She couldn't eat a bite.

After the meal, Rebel murmured to her, "You were going to show me around. How about now?"

She nodded, still not sure how she should take these latest revelations.

He took her hand and they sauntered outside to the back lawn and sat down side by side on the glider swing. His arm slipped around her and she leaned into him.

"This all seems like a fantasy," she said.

He grinned.

She turned up her face. "I do love you, Rebel, with all my heart, but about the alfalfa . . ."

He sealed her opening argument with a deep kiss that made her forget about everything else.

1 2

2010

2009

2007

2006

2005

2004

2003

2002

2001

2000